Praise for the Peggy Lee Garden Mysteries:

Pretty Poison:

"A Fantastic amateur sleuth." ~ The Best Reviews
"Smartly penned and charming garden mystery." ~
Romantic Times

Fruit of the Poisoned Tree:
"I can't recommend this book highly enough."~ Midwest
Book Reviews
"I love the world of Peggy Lee!" ~ Fresh Fiction

Poisoned Petals:
"Joyce and Jim are a fabulous team who create poignant,
entertaining mysteries." ~ The Best Reviews
"An enjoyable and cozy read." The Muse Book Reviews

Perfect Poison:
"A fabulous whodunit!" ~ Fresh Fiction
"You will enjoy this to no end! Highly recommended!" ~
Mystery Scene Magazine

A Corpse for Yew:

"Awesome story with good and rational twists! Love that it
tells about places I know! And there is some great plant
info at the same time!" ~ Snows Acre
"Joyce and Jim Lavene prove once again they are an
excellent writing team as they provide a quality regional
whodunit." ~ Harriet Klausner
A Thyme to Die:

"Totally enjoy this charac   Not only are
these good stories, but I l   nd
both their care and uses.
"There are plenty of tw   sing.
" ~ Cheryl Green

Peggy Lee Garden Mysteries

Pretty Poison
Fruit of the Poisoned Tree
Poisoned Petals
Perfect Poison
A Corpse For Yew
Buried by Buttercups—Novella
A Thyme to Die

Renaissance Faire Mysteries

Wicked Weaves
Ghastly Glass
Deadly Daggers
Harrowing Hats
Treacherous Toy
Perilous Pranks—Novella
Murderous Matrimony

Missing Pieces Mysteries

A Timely Vision
A Touch of Gold
A Spirited Gift
A Haunting Dream
A Finder's Fee

Taxi for the Dead Paranormal Mysteries

Broken Heart Ghoul
Undead by Morning – Short Story – Ebook only

Lethal Lily

By

Joyce and Jim Lavene

Book coach and editor—Jeni Chappelle
http://www.jenichappelle.com/

Dieffenbachia
Also known as dumb cane, this versatile houseplant releases poisonous crystals that are harmful to dogs and cats. Chewing on or swallowing this plant will result in swelling of the lips, mouth, and upper airway, making it difficult to breathe or swallow.

Chapter One

It was after midnight. Peggy Lee had been waiting in the dark parking lot of Tri-State Mini-Storage for more than an hour.

Since she was trying to keep a low profile, she hadn't looked at her phone or listened to music. There was still a light in the office. She knew someone was working.

A sign flapped in the warm breeze that blew up from a tropical storm churning at the Atlantic coast. She glanced at her watch again for the third time in as many minutes.

Where was Harry?

Peggy had only met Harry Fletcher a few days ago. They'd both received emails from her online friend, Nightflyer, suggesting they should work together.

A friend of mine is investigating an old murder in Charlotte and might call on you for help. I sent him to you because he knows part of the puzzle surrounding John's death. I'll speak with you when I can. ~ Nightflyer

The note had caught her attention—and held it. It had only been a few months since she'd learned that her late husband, John Lee, might have been deliberately murdered as part of an undercover operation he was on with the FBI.

She still wasn't sure it was true, but she'd decided to check into it.

John had been a Charlotte, North Carolina police detective when he'd been killed more than a decade ago. He'd been called out on a domestic abuse situation, not even a call he should have taken, but it was on his way home, and he'd gone willingly because he was needed.

The call went bad when the man, who'd been shooting at his wife's boyfriend, decided to shoot at the police. He'd escaped in the gunfight that ensued, but John had been killed. The shooter disappeared. John's partner had been at Peggy's door a few minutes later with the terrible news.

She pushed the thoughts of that night out of her head. It was a long time ago, but it still haunted her. She'd moved on with her life, but there was still pain remembering that night. Nothing would ever change that. She wouldn't let herself be trapped in the past—still she wanted to know what had *really* happened to John.

Her phone rang, startling her. She almost dropped it in her haste to answer. "Yes?"

"I've found the storage unit," Harry Fletcher whispered. "I forgot the bolt cutters on the floor of the car. Can you bring them? I'm at Unit 34."

She agreed to do it, and sighed. The man was terminally careless. He was always dropping or forgetting something. She wondered how he'd managed to stay alive while he'd worked as a private detective for so many years.

Harry said he'd been working as an informant for the FBI when John was killed. He bragged about all the side jobs he'd done with the Feds as they'd discussed the situation over iced tea in a sunlit atrium high above uptown Charlotte. Exotic lilies perfumed the cool air and fleet-footed waiters continually checked their glasses.

It wasn't the setting to discuss murder, yet that was what they'd come to do.

Peggy hadn't wanted to bring him to her house—it was better if she was the only one who knew about Harry. If her son, Paul, knew she was involved in asking questions about his father's death, he'd want to be part of it. She didn't want that to happen. His peace had been hard-won after John's death. He'd struggled with the knowledge that no one had been arrested in the case, eventually becoming a police officer himself. Paul had always said there was something wrong about John's shooting.

It seemed as though he might be right.

Harry claimed John had been working with the FBI on an undercover job when he was killed. He said the gunfight at the house was staged specifically to kill her husband because he had information he was supposed to turn over to another agent that night. He never made the meet. Whatever John knew was lost with him, according to Harry.

Maybe what Harry said was true—Peggy wasn't completely convinced. No one else was actively looking into John's death. She'd known about the FBI connection, but even that was recent. At the time of his death, no one mentioned it to her.

It was enough to keep her moving deeper into the plot, wondering what other secrets were out there, but she tried to keep her wits about her.

All the questions about John's death swirled around his involvement with the FBI that terrible night. It wasn't like John to keep secrets, but he hadn't told her about the FBI before he was killed. Even his partner hadn't known. Maybe he had no choice, or didn't want to worry her. She was willing to allow for possibilities, if they made sense.

Harry, being Harry, couldn't verify any of it. He'd left the files that could prove his accusations in a storage unit and forgotten them—until he'd received a letter saying the unit was going to be auctioned for lack of payment.

Stowing her handbag in the trunk of her car, Peggy grabbed the bolt cutters, locked the car, and headed the way she'd seen Harry go.

She didn't like how this was unfolding. Too much of it was out of her control. Harry was haphazard and sloppy in what he did. Parking in the back of the storage lot to wait until dark so the management wouldn't see him retrieve his possessions was probably illegal. From what Harry had told her of himself, it wasn't unusual for him to skirt the edge of the law.

Peggy wasn't so worried about doing something that might not be exactly legal, but didn't want to get herself in trouble over nothing. If there were answers, she wanted them. She just didn't trust Harry.

He had a dubious past. A quick Internet search showed he'd been jailed for burglary, theft, carrying concealed weapons without a license, trespassing—you name it. There were worse accusations that couldn't be proved. His shady past had followed him everywhere he went from North and South Carolina to New York. She could only imagine what she might have found if she'd had someone from the police department run a complete background search.

As she walked, tiny feet skittered at the sides of the buildings. She'd seen the big rattraps earlier when it was still light. Lucky she wasn't a squeamish person. Working in the garden with moles, voles, mice, and squirrels had made her immune to such creatures. She even admired spiders and ants.

It was the sound of human feet that worried her. She flattened herself against one of the walls from Row A and waited to see if it was Harry. Whoever it was walked quickly by, wheezing a little.

Not Harry.

Peggy continued down the narrow path between the plain white rows. Each unit was self-contained with dozens of various-sized doors that led into different-sized storage spots. She wished she could use the flashlight she'd brought, but she was afraid someone might notice from the office. She had to peer closely at every few units.

Unit 26. Not too much further.

Harry had told her that he'd stored all of his files here while he was on the run some years back. He'd been out of town a while and forgot that he was supposed to pay the monthly fee. He still didn't have the funds to ransom his belongings. Peggy had loaned him money, but he couldn't persuade the owner to work with him. She'd tried to pay the back rent too, but was told the auction day was set and wouldn't be changed.

That was how the crazy plan was born.

Harry said he still had the key for the unit, and knew 'someone' who got him a valid pass code to get through the gate. He said they could get in and take the files they needed if they sneaked in.

They agreed to help each other. Peggy would get the information Harry had about John's death—and she would help him find out what had really happened to Harry's wife, Ann.

Harry claimed that Ann had been murdered in their apartment—poisoned—twenty years ago. He'd come home to find her unconscious on the kitchen floor. She'd stopped breathing before emergency services could get there. They'd been unable to revive her.

He claimed he'd told the Charlotte police his theory, but they'd refused to investigate the death as anything but an accident. There were no signs of foul play. It appeared as though Ann had stepped off a stepladder and hit her head on the counter. It was tragic, but accidents happen.

According to Harry, this was the beginning of all the bad luck that had befallen him. He'd tried to investigate Ann's death, but had ended up unable to disprove the report the police had filed. A short time later, he left the area, only returning for occasionally for work.

Because Peggy was an expert in botanical poisons, their mutual acquaintance, Nightflyer, thought they were a perfect fit. She wasn't sure what she could do to investigate a twenty-year-old poisoning, but she was willing to try.

Harry's reasons for believing his wife's death was caused by poison were sketchy. Again, he said the facts were in the storage unit. He swore he wanted answers about his wife as much as Peggy wanted answers about John. She'd believed him—but she was beginning to wonder if their deal was as bogus as Harry himself.

Her cell phone buzzed in her pocket.

"Where are you?" Harry's voice was desperate.

"I'm trying to find *you*," she responded, frustrated. "There's someone else walking around out here in the dark."

"Hurry! They do a drive-through on a golf cart at 12:30. We have to get inside before they see us."

"Thanks for telling me!" She turned off her phone and put it back in her pocket after checking the time: 12:30 a.m. Another detail Harry had forgotten to mention.

She heard the golf cart start up. It was a large facility. She thought it would take a while to drive through the whole thing. With any luck, she'd reach Harry before the golf cart got close to them.

Peggy's foot brushed a pot on the side of one of the units. The pale light from one of the units showed her it was a tiny dieffenbachia set with some kind of colorful swizzle stick. Someone had probably received it for a gift and then left it out there to die. People were so careless with plants, as though they weren't living things.

She stuffed the decorative pot into the pocket of her jacket. There was bound to be someone who would want it.

The golf cart was headed in her direction, the bright light sweeping across the flat-topped buildings. If it got too close, the driver would see her. She had to reach Unit 34 before that happened.

Unit 30. Unit 32. She was getting closer.

She heard a car come through the main gate. The facility was open 24-hours. No doubt customers came and went at odd times. Headlights flashed through the property, but seemed to head in another direction. She was safe for the moment.

Unit 34.

Peggy stopped and looked around. There was no sign of Harry. Maybe he'd had to hide to stay away from the person on the golf cart. She put the bolt cutters down for a moment to take out her cell phone. What in the world was he doing now?

Before she could punch the call button by Harry's name, bright lights flashed in her eyes, and a loud voice said, "This is the Charlotte/Mecklenburg Police. Put your hands on your head, and kneel on the pavement."

Norfolk Island Pine
Araucaria heterophylla is a distinctive conifer, and a member of the ancient family, Araucariaceae. It is not a true pine. The tree comes from Norfolk Island in the Pacific Ocean between Australia, New Zealand, and New Caledonia. While this species grows as tall as any pine tree in its native land, it is sold at Christmas as a small sprout because of its shape.

Chapter Two

"She was here a few days ago. She wanted to pay the back fees on that unit." The manager of the storage facility was quick to point out her possible guilt. He was a large man with a stomach that rolled over his waistband. There was tomato sauce smeared on his white T-shirt.

"Okay." The officer taking his statement pulled at his cap in frustration. The manager had said much the same thing three or four times. "You'll have to come down to the station and file a formal complaint."

"I'll be glad to do that," the manager declared. "These creeps sneak in here and steal me blind all the time."

A second officer had helped Peggy to her feet after placing a plastic restraint around her wrists. He walked her to the backseat of the squad car and carefully nudged her inside.

Peggy was silent. She knew better than to try to defend herself. She hadn't really done anything wrong. The camera at the gate would show Harry punching in his code. He owned the storage unit, as far as she was willing to admit.

True, they'd been in *her* car—which was still somewhere on the lot. She wasn't volunteering that information. If she was lucky, she could still avoid having it towed to the impound lot. She knew from experience that getting a car out of impound was expensive.

She was fortunate that neither of the officers knew her. With Paul on the job, and many officers still on duty who knew John, she was well acquainted with members of the police department. Not being recognized was a plus toward getting away with being caught here. The fewer people who could identify her, the better. She wasn't as worried about the police officers who didn't know her or what would happen to her.

She was a tiny bit uneasy about explaining everything to Al McDonald, John's old partner, and to her husband—not to mention Paul.

Her plan at that moment was to call Harry as soon as she got to the station, lose her temper, and insist that he come to bail her out of jail. She had a very good lawyer who knew how to keep her mouth shut. With any luck, she'd be processed and out in time for breakfast, without her family or friends knowing what had happened.

The most they could charge her with was a misdemeanor anyway. That wouldn't affect her status as a contract forensic botanist with the police department. In all, it didn't look too bad for her. She just had to stay patient. And quiet.

But it was going to be hell for Harry when she was done with him.

As the police car rolled slowly out of the storage lot, she looked out the window, wondering where he'd disappeared. The police had confiscated the bolt cutters, so he wouldn't be able to get anything more done that night. They'd have to figure out a new plan to get the files before they were auctioned.

She sat back as the car reached the city street. Even though it was late, there were lights everywhere. Peggy had lived in Charlotte since she'd married John Lee right out of college. That was more than thirty years ago.

Back then, the city was much smaller, quieter, and definitely not as well lit. She liked it better the way it had been—before the modern skyscrapers had replaced the older buildings that had carried so much charm and elegance.

But it wasn't a bad city. Certainly not as bustling as Atlanta.

She'd been raised on a farm outside Charleston, South Carolina. Peggy had thought of moving back there after John had been killed. Paul had been insistent on staying. He was still in school, and hadn't wanted to leave his friends.

Her parents had sold their farm a few years back, and moved to Charlotte to be closer to the only family they had left. Now Paul was married—and about to be a father for the first time. She definitely wasn't going anywhere.

"We're getting out here." The same officer that had guided her into the car helped her out. He walked her into the police building and took off the plastic restraints when they reached the booking window.

"Name?" The grizzled sergeant at the desk asked, not looking up from his battered, gray computer.

"Margaret Hughes Lee." Peggy knew the sergeant. She hadn't seen him in a few years, but she and John had gone to his daughter's wedding. She hoped using her full name might throw off off—if he didn't look up.

"Address?"

"1421 Queens Road, Charlotte."

"Are you a U.S. citizen?"

"Yes."

The sergeant eyed her. Peggy contemplated a shriveled Norfolk Island pine on his desk.

"*Peggy?*" His nasal voice was incredulous. "Is that *you*?"

"Hi Don." She smiled at him. "How is Samantha? You know this poor little pine could do with some water."

"Samantha?" He took off his glasses and rubbed his eyes. "Is this some kind of joke? Is someone playing a prank? Because if they are, it's in poor taste at this time of morning."

She sighed. "I'm so sorry. It's not a joke. More like a mistake. If you could book me, and keep it under your hat, I'd appreciate it. There's no reason for everyone to know."

"You're kidding, right?"

"No. Not really. The charge is only a misdemeanor. Just put me in the system, but don't tell anyone."

* * *

Peggy sat on a bench for about forty-five minutes as hookers and drug dealers were brought in, charged with their crimes, and dispersed to jail cells.

Why couldn't that have happened to *her*?

She hadn't been restrained again, and no one looked twice at her. They'd given her cell phone and keys back. She knew what was coming, and wished it was already over. She had a lot of pent up rage that was waiting for Harry.

Finally, a tall black man with muscular shoulders and a bulbous nose was buzzed through the door from the main part of the police station. He wore a tired expression on his middle-aged face and a golf shirt with trout on it.

Al McDonald had been John's best friend growing up. They'd gone to college and had joined the police academy together. Al had been John's partner for twenty years. It had been Al who'd brought news of John's death to Peggy.

"Al—"

"Not here." He took her arm, and they went into a

small room that smelled like disinfectant. It was used for lawyers to meet with their clients. He closed the door behind them. "Take a seat, Peggy."

She was ready to deal with Al. She'd known Don had called him as soon as he'd refused to book her. She knew what she wanted to say, and she knew how he'd take it.

What she wasn't ready for was the door opening again to allow her husband to enter the small room too.

Steve Newsome had a dazed expression on his handsome face. His brown hair was rumpled from sleep, jeans and T-shirt hastily thrown on. They'd only been married a few years—almost still newlyweds.

She sat at the table, and fixed her eyes on Al. "You had to call Steve?"

Peggy felt like a small girl again—called on the carpet for something she'd done wrong. She didn't like the feeling. She was a grown woman, nearly sixty, for goodness sake. She didn't have to check with the men in her life before she made a move.

"Peggy." Al sighed and shook his head.

"Is my father on his way too?" She knew her insolent tone would rattle these two important men in her life. She didn't care.

"This is serious business." Al got off his feet by sitting in one of the hardback chairs. He'd been a beat cop, as John had, for many years. Both of them had fallen arches before they'd made detective.

She rolled her expressive green eyes. "It's *barely* a misdemeanor. I wasn't even holding the bolt cutters when the police arrived."

"Are you listening to yourself?" Steve demanded. "You were trespassing and caught attempting to break into a storage unit."

"I wasn't trespassing. I was with someone who had a code to get in the main gate and a key for the unit. I wasn't *attempting* to do anything. I was just standing there."

"Who were you with?" Steve asked.

"I'd rather not say." She studied her cuticles.

"We have you red-handed. The storage manager wants to press charges," Al grunted. "I can't even believe I'm saying this to you."

"Everyone needs to slow down and take a deep breath." Peggy did as she advised them to make her point. "Have the manager look at the videotape at the gate. That should make it clear that I was there with one of people who rent their units."

"The manager says the password your *friend* used to get in was fake. It was thrown out of the system a month ago. The unit you were trying to break into was confiscated for not paying the bill," Al said. "The manager also said you tried to bribe him into letting you have the contents of that same storage unit before the auction. Anything you'd like to say about that?"

"Yes." She got to her feet, shaking back her red hair that was tinged with white. "Are you planning to waterboard me? If not, I'm not telling you what I've been doing. I have the right to some privacy."

Steve nodded. "Unless you get busted—which you have. Who's the accomplice who helped you get into the mini-storage? Why were you there tonight?"

Peggy folded her arms across her chest. "If I'm not being charged, I'm going home. It's been a long night."

Al sat back and rubbed his big hand across his face. "You have always been one of the most *stubborn* women I've ever known."

She smiled. "Right up there with Mary, right?" Mary was his wife of many years.

"That's right." Al got up too. "And that's who I'm going home to right now. I know when I'm being stonewalled. Goodnight, Steve. She's all yours. I'll see you later."

Peggy was relieved that she wasn't being charged, even if it would have been simple to beat the charges than to explain them to Al and Steve. "Don't worry so much. I know what I'm doing."

Al hugged her, his eyes red-rimmed from lack of sleep. "Yeah. That's what worries me. You almost made poor Don have a heart attack. If you plan on getting arrested again, go to another town."

Once Al had left, Peggy knew the worst was yet to come. Even though she was ready to go, her car was still at the storage lot. That meant she had to ride home with Steve.

"Looks like it's just you and me now." He turned to her. "Where do you want to talk about this?"

English Ivy

English ivy belongs to the ginseng family and can be poisonous, if consumed. English ivy has overcome many obstacles to thrive in many countries. It will choke out other plants using hairy rootlets to tightly adhere to rough surfaces. Seeds are spread by birds.

Chapter Three

Peggy decided she wanted breakfast at the Waffle House—anything not to go home yet. Besides, she *was* a little hungry. It had been a long night.

Steve didn't seem to care where they talked. They walked out to his car that was parked in front of the station. He opened the door and held it for her. She felt like she was getting into another situation she didn't want to be in.

In the meantime, Harry was getting away, unscathed, when he should have been taking the heat with her. She longed to yell at him about his stupid, clumsy way of doing things.

First, she had to get through this with Steve.

"Where's your car?" He checked the area before he got in. "Impound lot?"

She raised her chin. "No. I left it at the mini-storage. I'll pick it up tomorrow."

He didn't start the car, instead staring out the window with his hands on the steering wheel. "Am I missing something? Am I doing something wrong, Peggy?"

"I don't know what you mean." She was about to go through the guilt wringer.

"Why didn't you trust me with this? Why didn't you tell me what was going on instead of going off on some hare-brained scheme where you could've been hurt?"

Peggy took a deep breath. She hated this part most of all. "Can't we decide that sometimes our business and personal lives are going to be separate?"

"Is this business or personal?"

"Business, of course. This is part of something I'm looking into. You do things with the FBI that I can't know about. Sometimes I have to do things that you don't know about."

"Seriously?" His anguished brown eyes pinned her. "Because I can't see where this involves gardening, your shop, teaching, or forensic work with the medical examiner."

She stared back—not wanting to hurt him or argue with him. But she was going to do this, whether he liked it or not. "It doesn't involve any of those things, Steve. It involves what happened the night John was killed. You said yourself that he may have been killed because of the work he was doing with the FBI. I met a man who might know what happened. I'm doing what I can to figure it out."

Steve was the one who'd told her about John working with the FBI. John had been working with him as his contact. "Who is this mystery man? Why didn't he come forward after John's death?"

"He said he did, but no one would listen."

"His name? I know the people involved."

"Harry Fletcher." In a way, telling Steve about Harry might be for the best. He might know something about Harry that could explain why he was so messed up. After last night, Peggy thought that information could be helpful in keeping her out of jail—or worse.

"The private detective?" Steve looked surprised. "How did you meet him?"

"He contacted me." She didn't tell him about Nightflyer. Steve disliked her online friend more than Paul did. "He wants my help trying to figure out what happened to his wife. Harry believes she was poisoned here in Charlotte about twenty years ago."

"That's right." Steve collected his thoughts. "That's why he agreed to work as an informant for us. He was trying to get some help. Didn't the police decide it was an accident?"

"Yes," she agreed. "But I can't tell you how many times poisonings are actually murder, and the police can't tell the difference."

"I think I've read those statistics." He frowned. "I don't remember Harry ever having much real information. What's he telling you that he knows about John's death?"

"That's why we were at the storage unit. All of his files are about to be auctioned. He said a lot of what he knows is in the files."

"And you never thought to come to me with this information—even though you know I'm interested in finding out what happened to John too."

Steve had a stake in what Harry said he had on the case—she agreed with him on that. The case was still open with the FBI, and she knew Steve felt at least partially responsible for John's death.

She hadn't told him because it felt odd discussing John's death with him. Maybe she was just being overly sensitive, but being married to Steve and discussing her late husband's death with him was really awkward.

Peggy compromised so that she didn't leave Steve hanging. "I didn't want to involve anyone else until I had some real answers. So far, all I have are promises that there are answers. That's not much for the FBI, or the police, to get involved with."

He reached across the seat and put his arms around her. "And you don't want Paul to find out, right? I understand. I won't say anything to him. But you have to promise me that you'll be more careful. I don't think Harry Fletcher is dangerous, but what if the storage manager had shot you instead of calling the police?"

She let him think it was all about Paul, instead of him. She wasn't happy about Paul finding out what she was doing either, but *that* was different.

"Then we probably wouldn't be going to the Waffle House." She was flip about it because she didn't know what to say. They probably should have a *real* conversation about it, but she didn't know where to start.

"That's for sure." He kissed her. "You know, I have to eat at those places on the road all the time."

"They have the *best* waffles." She smiled, trying to distract them both. "I have a waffle maker somewhere in my kitchen, but you don't want to eat a waffle *I* make from scratch."

He moved away from her, and started the car. "Waffle House it is."

* * *

The Waffle House was nearly empty. A waitress in a pink uniform with a nametag that said, 'Candy' on it, came up to them quickly with two cups of coffee. Peggy asked for tea, and they each ordered a waffle.

When they were alone, Steve took Peggy's hands in his. "Would you like me to go with you to see Harry? It doesn't have to be official. I'm your worried husband. I don't have to be there as an FBI agent interested in the case."

"In other words, I could head out with the full—though unofficial—weight of a large national security organization at my back?" She laughed. "That *might* spook him! I can handle Harry, even though I might be arrested for his murder before it's over. He's kind of crazy and has no idea what he's doing."

"I remember him that way too."

"But I promise to call if I need your help."

He looked skeptical. "You didn't call me before you went 'undercover' last night."

"Well, now our organizations are working together. I promise to call you—if you promise not to overreact every time something unplanned happens. I've been doing this kind of thing for a long time."

"You mean getting arrested, almost killed—that kind of thing?" His smile was doubtful.

"Exactly."

Their waffles arrived, with Peggy's tea, and they talked about normal things for a while. There were roofers working on their turn-of-the-century home. They'd both been surprised to wake up and find them there one morning a few days before.

The three-story, twenty-five room house in Myer's Park didn't belong to Peggy. She'd lived there with John, who'd inherited it, but it would never belong to Paul. Now, she and Steve were there until John's cousin decided to take possession of it. The house was maintained as part of a trust by the Lee family.

The family wasn't happy about Peggy living there now that John was dead, but it was pointless for the house to remain empty. John's young cousin who'd inherited it traveled extensively as part of his job and had no plans to settle down in the near future. He'd asked Peggy to stay put so there was someone living there.

Peggy loved the old house and wanted to live there as long as she could. Her basement was filled with her plant experiments, and her foyer had a large blue spruce growing in it. It was the perfect house for her. She secretly hoped she'd die there, and they'd take her out with a sheet across her head, so she wouldn't see herself leaving.

But being an old house, it had a lot of maintenance that had to be done. One of the problems right now was the roof. As the work was being done, the roofers had begun complaining about the English ivy growing across the old shingles.

The plant was beautiful, but it could be invasive too. Twining tendrils and roots excreted a sticky substance that made it possible for the plant to climb on anything. Trying to get it off where it was the thickest had turned out to be a difficult job that had made the roofers want to charge extra.

They were pushing to spray the roof and walls with herbicide, and kill the ivy. Peggy was totally against the practice since it would kill all the other plants in close proximity to the house. With the difference in price, John's uncle, Dalton Lee—who was responsible for the house—wanted to do whatever the roofers wanted. It had been an ongoing battle.

"How bad could it be to use an herbicide?" Steve poured more syrup on his waffle.

"How bad?" Peggy stared at him over her cup. "Some of the rose bushes and azaleas close to the house are over a hundred years old. You can't find those breeds anymore. They can't be replaced. It would be devastating."

"Okay." He smiled. "Sorry. Just that you and Dalton are formidable foes. I don't see either of you winning."

"Dalton knows it would be a mistake. He doesn't understand the value of plants, but he understands the value of the house." She picked up her fork. "Besides, I'm going to talk to Sam about it today. I know he's done this before. There must be something that could make the job go faster without killing everything."

Sam Ollson was her partner at her garden shop, The

Potting Shed. He took care of the landscaping end of the business.

Peggy tried calling Harry again while Steve paid for breakfast. There was still no answer.

Why bother having a phone if you never answered it?

Peony
The peony is a flowering plant native to Asia, Southern Europe, and Western North America. Most are herbaceous perennial plants, but some are the size of small trees. The peony is named after Paeon, a student of the Greek god of medicine. Zeus saved the student from the wrath of Asclepius, his teacher, by turning him into the peony flower. Research continues into more than 262 compounds obtained from the plants.

Chapter Four

Steve drove them home after leaving the Waffle House. Neither of them thought it was a good idea to get Peggy's car until morning. By that time, maybe things would have calmed down at the mini-storage.

Peggy hoped a different manager would be on duty.

"I have to be there for the auction tomorrow anyway." Peggy closed the car door and walked toward the house. She could hear her Great Dane, Shakespeare, barking loudly from inside. She hoped it didn't wake her neighbors. "I'll have one of the kids at the shop drive me over there."

"Or I could take you."

"There's no reason to upset your schedule because I made a mistake."

"I don't mind."

She opened the kitchen door at the side of the house, and Shakespeare ran full-tilt into her. If he hadn't pushed her into Steve, she would've fallen on the ground under his weight.

Peggy had rescued Shakespeare from an abusive owner

and loved him dearly, but his joyous welcomes could be a bit much.

"You missed me, didn't you?" She stroked his floppy, unclipped ears, and massive black muzzle. "You might need to start missing me a little *less*."

Shakespeare's big brown eyes were focused completely on her, until he saw the door close behind her, and galloped off in the other direction. He wasn't used to his humans going in and out at all times of the day and night.

"It's only two a.m." Steve glanced at his watch and yawned. "I'm going back to bed. What about you?"

"I'm much too nervous and upset to sleep." She put her handbag, and the tiny dieffenbachia in her pocket, on the kitchen table. "You go on up. I'm going to take a look at my plants."

He put his arms around her. "Maybe we could find something *else* to do with all that nervous energy." He kissed her. "And I could talk you into letting me take you to the mini-storage tomorrow."

She smiled and leaned against him. "That *does* sound more interesting than looking at my plants right now. What did you have in mind?"

* * *

Peggy fell asleep in Steve's arms for about an hour. Then her restless mind woke her and urged her to get out of bed.

She groaned when she saw it was only four a.m. She'd hoped it was closer to six. *Oh well.* Still time to check on her plants in the basement. Peggy got up and pulled on a gray sweatshirt and sweatpants. She studied Steve's sleeping face for a moment. He was so handsome and kind.

Funny how things could change. After John had died, she thought she would always be alone. She'd told herself that she didn't mind. She'd had her love. Then Steve had sneaked into her life, and her heart. He'd brought light and love, changing her life again.

Shakespeare accompanied her down the spiral staircase from her bedroom to the first floor. She loved the feel of the cool marble stairs against her feet, and brushed her hand against a branch of the blue spruce that grew beside the stairs. The scent filled the air around her.

She loved the big, old house when it was quiet. It made settling sounds, like an old tree in the forest. She'd managed to leave her mark on it—something she wasn't sure was possible when she'd first arrived as a young bride. So many generations of John's family had added to the rambling halls and rooms. She'd expected to get lost in it, but it never happened.

Some of the old furniture in the library, dining room, and bedrooms had been handmade by John's grandfather. The antique rose china had come from John's great-grandmother. The piano had been brought by ship from New York in 1920, pulled by horse and wagon from the port of Wilmington to Charlotte.

Peggy knew her contribution to the house could mostly be found in the grounds surrounding it. She'd planted trees and bushes, landscaped the old roses, and added terraces and other outside features. She felt sure no one in the future would quibble with the work she and John had accomplished in their lifetimes.

John had been an avid gardener too. Except for her specific field of study—poisonous botanicals—he could keep up with her on any gardening projects. He'd created the circular stone terrace and fountain and then filled it with tulips, hyacinths, and daffodils. He'd made beautiful benches that graced the walkways.

She missed the understanding and appreciation of gardening that they had shared for thirty years. Many times, it was the last thing they'd talked about at night and were eager to get started on a project in the morning.

It wasn't something she and Steve had in common. He was good about listening to her ramble on about a new rose or peony, but she knew it wasn't where his heart was. She smiled when she remembered how puzzled his face had been when they'd first met, and she'd started talking about various plants. He was better educated now.

Peggy was about to go into the basement, where she kept her botanical experiments, when the phone in her pocket rang.

"Mom!" Paul's voice was high-pitched and excited. "We're leaving for the hospital. Mai says it's time."

"We'll meet you there."

Paul had already hung up before she could say goodbye. Peggy smiled, remembering the night he'd been born. She'd thought John was going to drive *into* the hospital when they couldn't find a close parking space.

She ran upstairs excitedly and kissed Steve. "Wake up! We're about to be grandparents."

* * *

Three hours later, the hospital staff was sending Mai back home. She wasn't dilating enough. The doctor said she wasn't having real contractions.

"But we're getting ready for the big event," he said with a broad grin on his face.

"Sorry to drag you out for nothing," Paul said to Steve and Peggy. "I thought for sure she'd know when the baby was coming since she works for the medical examiner's office. She knows everything about *dead* bodies."

Peggy laughed. "It happens to a lot of people, no matter what their training. Even doctors and nurses are fooled. It's a huge moment in your life. It's easy to get carried away."

Mai stepped out of the cubicle, wearing her street

clothes instead of a hospital gown. Her pretty, almond-colored face was annoyed. "I feel like a bloated idiot."

"You're not any kind of idiot." Peggy hugged her. "And maybe this is just as well since your parents are in Europe. I know they want to be here too."

"Thanks. I wish that made me feel better." Mai wiped tears from her dark eyes. "I just want to get this over. I'm sorry I decided to take a leave of absence from the ME's office before the baby was born. I'm so bored. All I want to do is eat and sleep."

Paul put his arm around her shoulder and rubbed her large tummy. "It's going to happen any time now. Just be patient. Besides, we didn't want the baby to be around all those chemicals and see dead bodies."

Mai faced him with no humor in her expression. "The baby has been around those chemicals for the last nine months. She knows as much about forensics as I do. Let's go home. I need to stop at Krispy Kreme on the way. And don't say anything to me about gaining weight."

"Goodnight, you two." Steve smiled. "I guess we'll try this again later."

"Sorry again." Paul rubbed his head. "Any herb she could take to get the baby out sooner, Mom?"

"Not a good idea," Peggy told him. "Let nature take its course. She'll be all right."

Paul glanced at Mai's retreating back. "I guess I better go. She'll leave me here. That woman is single-minded right now when it comes to food."

Steve laughed as Paul ran after his wife. "You know, I thought the whole thing about cravings was a myth."

"You'd find out different at your own peril." She took his arm. "At least it's morning. I'm glad *that* night is over."

"Me too. Now we can go home and really get the day started."

"I'd like to get a do-over on it." She yawned.

"What are you planning for today—besides getting

your car back?"

"We're bringing in fall stock at the store. I know it's still summer, but people have to plan ahead for their spring gardens. Those tulips and hyacinths don't plant themselves."

"Unless you hire Sam."

"That's right. Another good reason to plan ahead. Sam is very popular. And *very* busy in the fall."

They went back to the house—and another crazy welcome from Shakespeare. Steve took the dog for a walk while Peggy made tea and coffee. A few minutes later, two agents who worked with Steve showed up. It had become routine a few days a week for them to get started here.

Peggy liked Agent Millie Sanford. She was a very competent redhead who was calm, smart, and funny. It made her feel good that Millie had Steve's back if they ever ran into trouble.

Agent Norris Rankin was another story. He and Peggy had rubbed each other the wrong way since they'd met. Peggy found him generally condescending and obnoxious. Steve trusted him though, so she did the best she could to get along with the man.

This morning, Peggy's neighbor, Walter Bellows, ended up around their table in the kitchen too. "Did something happen last night that caused your dog to bark at odd hours?"

Steve was bringing Shakespeare in as Walter arrived. The dog almost spun the man around as he raced by him to get to his food that Peggy had put out.

"Nothing I want to talk about." Peggy got mugs for her visitors. "If you're not busy though, I wouldn't mind a ride to the shop today."

"I can drive you," Steve said.

"Maybe not," Norris countered. "We had another

burglary last night. We got the call at about 2 a.m. Antique jewelry again—this time diamonds. A woman was roughed up a little but not seriously hurt. I'm hoping we can finally get a description of the gang responsible for this."

"Why is the FBI looking into local burglaries?" Peggy wondered. "Shouldn't that be the Charlotte police?"

"The FBI has been following this gang of thieves through several states," Steve explained. "Right now, they're in Charlotte. I'd like to be the one to stop them."

Millie tossed her super-straight red hair. It was as fiery as Peggy's hair had been in her youth. "I think Steve could take the time to drop off his wife, Norris."

"Whatever." Norris closed his planner. "If that's what *you* want to do, Steve."

"I have no burglaries to look into, nor a single homicide to investigate." Walter poured himself a cup of coffee, liberally adding cream and sugar. "I'd be delighted to take Peggy to the shop."

He smiled at her, a short man who always wore a brown and black tweed cap that caused tufts of his gray hair to stick out all over his head. Peggy and Walter were neighbors who'd become friends with their shared love of plants.

Peggy smiled at Steve. "I'm good with Walter's offer to take me to the garden shop. Don't worry about it."

Steve frowned, but went along with the plan. They met upstairs as they were getting ready to go their separate ways. He zipped the back of her brown dress and kissed her. "You know, this doesn't have to be the way our work days start. I know you don't like Norris. I could have him and Millie start meeting me at the office every morning."

"That's okay." She touched up her hair, and put on a pair of jade and gold earrings. "I get to see you for a few minutes extra during the week this way. I can put up with Norris."

He hugged her tightly to him. "If you're sure. Be

careful today. I know you want whatever information is at the storage building. Someone else might want it too. Call me if you need *anything*."

"I will." She smiled, and kissed him again. "Don't be so worried. I can look after myself."

"I'd appreciate it if you said the actual words—*I'll call you if I need you, Steve.*"

She laughed at him. "You'd think I got you out of bed in the middle of the night because I'd been arrested or something."

"Peggy?"

"Okay." She stared seriously into his eyes. "I'll call you if I need you, Steve. All right?"

"All right."

They agreed to text each other during the day to decide if they wanted to eat dinner out that night. Steve went down first. He left right away, taking Norris and Millie with him.

Peggy went down a few minutes later, and found Walter helping himself to some leftover donuts that she'd bought from a high school student as part of a fundraiser.

"I'm afraid I need to ask a favor," she said to him.

"Anything, dear lady." The words were muffled around the chocolate-covered donut in his mouth.

"I need to make one stop before I go to The Potting Shed. You can leave me there. I can go to the shop once I pick up my car."

"*That's* what's missing." He clapped his hands together. "I knew it was something. What happened to your car?"

"I'll tell you on the way."

Peggy set the alarm for the house, glad to see the roofers hadn't arrived yet. She was hoping to get the answer she needed from Sam before they started working on getting rid of the English ivy again. She knew Dalton would take a shortcut, if he could. She also knew he'd regret it later.

She knew Steve had thought she was going right to the mini-storage, but she really planned to yell at Harry at his motel before they went there. Peggy knew Steve might get too involved in what they were doing if he was there for what was sure to be some unpleasant moments.

Even though she knew Harry didn't have a car, she figured they could take a cab to the mini- storage for the auction and then pick up her car. She probably wouldn't need a code to get on the lot during the auction—they were sure to leave the gate open.

She'd only been to Harry's room at the Flowers Motel once. It was a sleazy dive that was probably on the national bedbug list. She'd been careful not to sit on the chair or bed while she was there. The rest of their meetings had been at restaurants where she wasn't familiar, and spots in Charlotte that were easy to reach from the garden shop while she was working.

When she told Walter where she was going and why, he stared at her as though she'd lost her mind. "Seriously, Peggy, maybe you should have allowed Steve to bring you there—with an armed escort. There are dozens of shootings and drug dealers in that area."

"You don't have to stay, or even park. Just stop the car, and let me out. I know someone staying there. He and I need to have a discussion."

"This is about what happened to you last night, I assume." He started the older Bentley and carefully inched down the driveway toward Queens Road. "Is it wise to see this man again after he was responsible for your nearly being arrested?"

"It may not be wise, but I'm in the middle of it now. I'm going to see it through."

He shrugged and looked both ways at the oncoming traffic that was streaming toward them. When there were absolutely no cars or buses that he could see, he slowly crept out into the street.

Peggy took a deep breath. She could've probably ridden there faster on her bike. If she didn't have so much to do—and so many places to go—she would've done that. She was grateful that Walter was willing to give her a ride, but being patient was difficult sometimes.

Walter's Bentley chugged its way toward South Boulevard. He didn't like the Interstate highway and would do anything to avoid it. They drove into one of the most depressed business areas, and headed for the Flowers Motel.

The motel had once been an office building that had fallen into disrepair along with the rest of the property around it. Four men in their underwear sat outside at a street-level smoke shop in the warm morning air. They waved as the Bentley went by.

"I'm glad you don't require me to park in this place." Walter eyed the men suspiciously. "I'm afraid I'd have very little left of my car when I returned."

"Don't worry. I parked here. No one bothered my car."

He sniffed indignantly. "Madam, you drive a *hybrid*. This car is a classic. Comparing the two would be like comparing opera and pop music!"

Peggy smiled and ignored him. Walter liked to complain, but he had a very good heart. She knew he'd do almost anything for her. She felt the same about him.

"Right there." She pointed. "Number six on the ground floor. Just pull in there, and I'll get out."

He pulled the Bentley between the faded yellow parking lines and dared a glance around them. "Are you *sure* you want to do this?"

"Absolutely." She got out of the car and reached back for her handbag. "Thank you for the ride. Can you find your way back to Queens Road?"

"I can. Please be careful. I feel people watching us and plotting our demise." He shivered. "Your husband won't thank me for bringing you to your doom."

"He would've done the same thing," she assured him. "Be careful driving back."

Peggy left the Bentley and walked confidently to the door with the large brass 6 on it. She knocked, but there was no answer. She tried calling Harry again on the phone. Still no answer. She knocked, and yelled out his name, drawing unwanted attention from the men in their underwear across the parking lot from her.

Still no answer.

She finally put her hand on the doorknob and turned. The door eased open. Peggy stepped carefully into the room. The small bed was carelessly made. The TV was on with the news channel playing low. There was a light on in the bathroom, and the door was partially closed.

She walked across the tacky pink carpet, and tapped on the door. "Harry?"

No answer.

She *really* didn't want to open the bathroom door. Instead, she knocked hard, the thin door shaking under her onslaught. "Harry!"

Still no answer.

It wasn't like she hadn't seen naked men before. She knew he liked to drink. He might have fallen asleep in the tub.

Peggy slowly pushed open the door. Something was caught on the back of it. She had to shove to get it open. Eyes closed, she poked her head in through the partially open space.

When she peeked, she saw Harry lying on the floor, a broken glass near one hand. There was a bluish tinge to his face—his lips were colorless. White foam was coming from his mouth.

"Oh, Harry." She shook her head as she maneuvered around the door into the tiny room and crouched beside him. "What did you get mixed up in this time?"

Ginger
In 1585, Jamaican ginger was the first oriental spice to be grown in the New World and imported back to Europe. It has a history of cures in folk medicine including uses for nausea and vomiting, rheumatoid arthritis, and joint and muscle pain. Ginger also acts as a food preservative.

Chapter Five

"How do you know your friend has been poisoned?" the 911 operator asked.

"It's part of my job to know these things." Peggy walked out of the bathroom. "I'm a forensic botanist with the medical examiner's office."

"Yes, ma'am. I'll send help."

"Thank you." She put away her phone and stood at the bathroom door again, surveying the room.

"What happened to him?" Walter asked.

Peggy jumped, unnerved by his voice behind her. "I thought you were leaving." She put her hand to her chest as her heat beat slowed again.

"What kind of man would I be to leave you in this terrible place?" He gazed around the room. "It's even worse on the inside, if that's at all possible. Is that the man you were meeting?"

"Yes." She sighed. "It looks like I'm on my own again."

"Is he dead?" He sniffed. "I smell cheap scotch."

"Yes, he's dead. You probably smell what was in that glass." She pointed to the shattered glass. "It appears that he was poisoned."

"Poisoned? How can you tell?"

"There are the usual signs of toxicity. You see the white foam at his mouth, and the coloration of his face. No doubt he lost control of his body, and fell to the floor, dropping the glass he held. It probably still contains the poison that was used."

"Who would be that stupid?"

"You'd be surprised. Most poisonings are mistaken for heart attacks. Poisons mimic those symptoms. Secondary events, like hitting your head on something or being struck by a car, can be mistaken for cause of death. No one wants to do an expensive autopsy if they don't have to. In most cases the police go with what they see unless they have some plausible reason to look further into the death."

"Can you tell what type of poison was used?" Walter stroked his chin.

Peggy shook her head. "I'm not Sherlock Holmes. It'll take some careful analysis to determine what killed him, though I think it's odd that he thought his wife was poisoned too."

"I would imagine that would be uncommon."

She tried to observe the scene for evidence, as she'd been taught during her six-weeks of forensic training. She used that training, and her degree in botany, to help out at the medical examiner's office as a contract worker.

The crime scene wasn't exactly part of her expertise, but she'd picked up a lot working with the police. She wasn't really close to Harry so it was possible to be objective. She'd seen trained detectives with years of experience break down at the sight of a friend who'd been killed.

There was still shaving cream and a razor on the sink. It looked as though Harry was about to shave as he finished off his scotch. The piece of ginger she'd given him to chew on for stomach upset was still in a plastic bag.

There was no blood anywhere. No signs of a fight. He'd managed to avoid striking his head on the toilet, bathtub, or sink when he fell. It would have been an easy thing to do in that small space.

Police and emergency sirens were coming their way. Walter panicked. "Should we leave before they get here?"

"Of course not. I work with the police. I can help with the crime scene. Look around for a bottle of scotch."

"What about the first person on the scene being accused of the crime?" Walter's gaze darted around the room. "I've seen that on television."

"A real crime scene investigation is different." Peggy didn't see a bottle of scotch—empty or partial—anywhere out in the open. She didn't want to search in places where she'd have to disturb potential evidence.

"They're here." Walter pointed to the police car that had pulled behind his Bentley. "I guess I won't be leaving right away. I shouldn't have come in. What was I *thinking*?"

"Relax. It's good that they're here," Peggy said as the police officers came into the motel room.

The investigating officer was a very nice young man named Spratt. He took a quick peek at Peggy's credentials from the ME's office. "I'll still have to ask you a few questions, Dr. Lee. A detective is on his way. He might have some questions too."

"Please pay attention to the scotch in the broken glass," she advised. "I think Harry Fletcher may have been poisoned. There should be a bottle in here somewhere. We need to find that too."

"Maybe you should come this way, ma'am. It might be best if you wait in the police car." Officer Spratt took off his hat and opened the back door to the car for her and Walter. "I'll be back in a few minutes to check on you."

"This is *not* good." Walter fussed. "We're going to be arrested."

"Don't be silly." She took out her phone and called Al. "We have valuable information they'll want for the investigation—at least *I* do. As soon as the detective gets here, I'm sure they'll let you go home."

Peggy got Al's voicemail. She left him a message and sat back to wait.

It occurred to her that this might be one of those times that Steve wanted to hear from her. She hated to bother him since there was nothing he could do. But she'd promised to call if something unusual came up. This definitely qualified. If she already ruined their new spirit of cooperation, Steve could get difficult again.

"Hi Peggy." he said as he answered the phone. "Is everything okay?"

"There's nothing wrong with me or Walter, but Harry's dead. Walter and I found him at the motel. We're waiting for Al, or some other homicide detective, to get here."

"I thought you were going to the shop. Where are you?"

She could hear voices talking to him. He was busy. He really didn't have time for a long explanation. "I'll explain later. There's nothing you can do to help, Steve. I didn't want to bother you, but you made me promise to call."

"Are you sure?"

"Absolutely. You know, I *do* work for the medical examiner from time-to-time. I'm not a novice at this. I think Harry may have been poisoned."

He was silent for a minute. "All right, Peggy. But keep me posted, okay? I love you."

"I will. Thanks. Love you too."

She smiled as she put the phone back in her bag. Steve was such a worrier. She loved that he cared what happened to her, but she could take care of herself, especially in a situation like this.

Two more police cars pulled up, followed by a plain brown Ford that needed a good wash.

"There's Al now," she said to Walter. "I told you it wouldn't be long."

"Make sure you tell him that I didn't see a thing until after you saw it. You were the first one on the scene, so to speak."

Al left his car and walked by where they were sitting. He did a comical double take when he saw Peggy and Walter in the backseat and opened the car door. "What's going on? What are you doing here?"

"Waiting for you." She smiled. "Didn't you get my message?"

He frowned. "You know I don't like to check the phone too often. Someone is always sending me a text or trying to call me. Were you letting me know that you were being arrested?"

"Of course not. We're witnesses."

"*I'm* not a witness," Walter denied. "I didn't even know the poisoned man."

Al's brows went up. "We know he's been poisoned, do we?" He waited while Peggy got out of the car. "Maybe you better walk me through this. Walter, I think you should wait here. You don't want to be messed up in it."

Walter complained and threatened to call his lawyer but stayed where he was.

Al ignored him. He and Peggy walked into the motel room together. "Who is the man in the motel?"

"His name is Harry Fletcher. He works as a private investigator."

"Those guys are always trouble," Al mumbled. "Tell

me how you happened to find him in this dump. Does it relate to you trying to break into the storage facility last night?"

Of course that meant telling him all about their investigation into John's death—things she hadn't wanted to share until she had some concrete evidence. She should've known it would all come out before she was ready.

"So Harry Fletcher, our dead man, told you he knew something we—as in the police and FBI—didn't know about John's death." Al summed up. "And you followed his lead to figure out what it was. That was damn stupid, Peggy. I know you know better than that. If there was anything else to know about John's death, don't you think I would've told you? I'm not holding anything back from you and Paul. You know what I know."

"Al, you said yourself that you didn't know John was working with the FBI at that time. There could be other things you didn't know. Harry said he knew some of those things. Wouldn't you have wanted to know too?"

He didn't answer that loaded question, and instead took a look at Harry's body. He had Officer Spratt call for the medical examiner. "I guess whatever this man knew, he took to his grave. You really think this was a poisoning?"

"I am. We'll have to check for various toxins. I told Officer Spratt to make sure he looked for a bottle of scotch."

Spratt shook his head. "So far, we haven't found any kind of bottle."

"Make sure you check the trashcans outside," Al said. "And send someone to talk to the motel manager."

"I had someone get a sample of the scotch on the floor," Spratt told him. "I'll give it to the medical examiner when she gets here."

"Good work." Al turned to Peggy. "Do you want to wait for Dorothy? You can fill her in on all of it."

"There's nothing more I can do here." She glanced at her watch. "I have to be somewhere else. Can you tell Dorothy what I told you? I'll talk to her later."

"You'll have to fill out some paperwork later too."

"I know. I'll take Walter with me."

"Good idea." He nodded. "I haven't forgotten about the break-in at the mini-storage. What were you and Harry Fletcher trying to find there?"

Peggy had to answer. "I'm going to the auction later. I'll tell you all about it."

"That's not what I wanted to hear. Don't get further involved in this until you talk it over with me," Al called out to her retreating form. "You hear me, Peggy?"

Crocus
There has been human cultivation of the crocus for more than 3,500 years. From China, to the Greeks and Romans, this colorful little flower has been valued through history. Stories say that Cleopatra of Egypt bathed in its essence before going to her lover. Saffron was used in teas and salves, to dye clothes and spice foods. The history of this little plant is the history of the human race as it has grown and thrived.

Chapter Six

"Where to now?" Walter asked. "Please tell me it isn't someplace rat and criminal-infested where we'll find another crime scene."

"There *was* once a murder at The Potting Shed," Peggy told him. "But it's more likely we'll find Sam unloading a truck filled with fall bulbs than a corpse."

"You never told me there was a murder at The Potting Shed. Was that a recent thing?"

"No. It was years ago, before Steve and I were married. In fact, I met Steve at around the same time. The murder was tragic. It involved poison—from the anemone bulb. I was scared half to death, but I got through it."

"You always do, don't you?" Walter turned on Church Street. "I'd like a sneak peek at those fall bulbs, since they've just arrived. There's a small area behind my house that would be perfect for spring flowers. I was thinking of some crocus, perhaps."

"You're welcome to check them out—if you want to help unload them. I might even give you a discount."

"I could be persuaded, if there's a big cup of tea from Emil's shop across the courtyard."

"I think that could happen."

Walter parked behind The Potting Shed, next to the large truck that was delivering supplies. Sam was driving their forklift in and out of the trailer as he moved bags of bulbs, potting soil, and fertilizer. He waved to Peggy and Walter before disappearing into the truck again.

"Come up this way." Peggy got out of the Bentley and took her handbag with her. She led Walter up a short flight of cracked concrete stairs to the back door of the shop.

"If I'm going inside the maw of the beast, do you have an apron or something I can put over my clothes?"

"I have gloves and aprons inside." She smiled at him. "Thanks for helping out."

"No. Thank *you* for doing anything to take my mind off that wretched dead man. I can't believe you choose to do this kind of thing. You're a refined, intelligent woman in most instances. Perhaps you should take up needlepoint or knitting as a hobby."

Peggy left him near the back door without replying to his taunts. She called Emil Balducci at the Kozy Kettle to order tea for them, and coffee for Sam. She had an apron, rubber boots, and gloves for herself. It paid to be prepared in the garden business.

"Morning, Peggy," Selena Rogers called from the front counter. "I was wondering if you were going to make it in today."

Selena was a student at Queens University—a former botany student of Peggy's. She'd accidentally taken her class—Peggy was still teaching at the time—and had fallen in love with plants. Her long black hair was pinned up on her head, emphasizing her cocoa-colored skin and golden eyes. She was tall and thin, a runner, though she'd given up track at school.

"I always try to be here for the start of a new gardening season." Peggy fed the large koi that lived in her indoor pond. "No matter how long I do this, it's always exciting."

"Yeah." Selena rolled her expressive eyes. "Sam was *really* excited about emptying that truck this morning. He had to send Tucker out on a job by himself."

"I'm sure Tucker can handle it. He's been working with Sam for a while. Sometimes we have to let the little birds leave the nest." Peggy tied her apron over her dress, and sat down in her rocking chair to replace her shoes with her boots.

"You know how Sam is—everything has to be perfect. He's so picky."

"That's what makes him good at his job."

"And a pain in the butt," Selena muttered.

"If there's no one here, you can come in back and help unload too. We can hear the door chime if anyone comes in."

"Sure. I'll be glad to do that. Just let me get the register set up. I hope it doesn't take too long. I'd hate to miss all that *excitement*."

"More hands make the job go faster," Peggy quoted. "Don't take too long."

Peggy smiled with pleasure as she walked through The Potting Shed. She loved the heart-of-pine floors that squeaked when she walked on them. The shop had plenty to offer the novice gardener as well as the experienced one. She was always searching for new products to tempt her customers who stopped by during their lunch breaks from banks and other offices nearby.

The Potting Shed was located in Brevard Court, at the doorway to Latta Arcade. The mini-mall was built in the early 1900s and preserved to perfection for shoppers. Outside the garden shop was a cobblestone courtyard with café-style tables and chairs for those who wanted to stroll between shops and eat lunch. Peggy and Sam maintained the plants in the courtyard so that each season held a different display with their shop's name on it.

She walked through the shop to the warehouse space in the back where they were able to store large items such as shovels, wheelbarrows, and bulk purchases of mulch and other items.

Walter was looking through the bags of new bulbs with all the eagerness of a cat stalking a mouse. He'd taken off his tweed hat and put on a green Potting Shed ball cap.

"Find anything interesting?" she asked.

He jumped. "I was about to give Sam a hand. I didn't want to get in his way."

"That's okay. Let's see what we can do to make this finish faster."

Sam brought several pallets of mulch off the truck with the forklift. He paused when he saw Peggy and Walter. "I was wondering if anyone was going to show up this morning," he yelled above the sound of the engine.

"Sorry," Peggy said. "I was detained."

"At a murder scene," Walter added. "The man was poisoned."

Sam raised his blond brows. He was a big man with large hands that loved digging in the dirt. His family had important plans for him when he was in school. Sam had thrown them all aside to become Peggy's partner in The Potting Shed. He was responsible for the growing landscape business.

"Sounds like fun. I can't wait to hear about it."

"How much more is coming off the truck?" Peggy asked him.

"This is the last big load. I need you two to get the smaller things while I get all of this stored away. I'll come help you in a minute."

Walter sized up Sam's broad shoulders and big chest, emphasized by his tight-fitting green T-shirt. "Perhaps I would be better at organization so that you could lift what's left in the truck."

Peggy grabbed Walter's arm. "Sorry. Sam knows how he wants everything back there. You're stuck with the grunt work like me. Don't forget—bulbs and tea when this is over."

"Yes. Of course." Walter sighed, tied on his apron, and followed her across the shaky ramp into the back of the truck.

"Those must be ours." Peggy pointed to pond supplies and boxes of seed. "Let's take those out."

They passed Selena on the ramp, and Peggy told her what to get. Sam checked off the supplies on his list as they were put in place. In about thirty minutes, they were pulling up the ramp, and the truck was leaving.

"I got you a coffee." Peggy smiled at Sam as they closed the loading doors.

"I hope it includes something to eat," he said. "I'm starving."

"You got *him* coffee?" Selena demanded. "No one ever gets *me* coffee."

"If you ever did any hard work," Sam replied, "She'd get you coffee too."

"I thought you'd already had coffee," Peggy said. "Of course I'll get you something too."

The two sniped at each other like brother and sister all the time, but Peggy couldn't imagine trying to run the shop without them. She called Emil and ordered croissants for everyone—plus another coffee for Selena.

While they waited for Emil and Sofia to bring the food from the Kozy Kettle Tea and Coffee Emporium, they sat outside on the edge of the loading dock. The morning was still cool, though afternoon temperatures were forecast to be in the high nineties.

"So you found another dead guy." Sam's blue eyes narrowed against the morning sun in his tanned face.

"He wasn't a stranger." Peggy filled him in on what had been going on with Harry Fletcher.

Selena took a quick breath. "Are you a suspect now?"

"No. Of course not." Peggy watched the after-rush-hour traffic flow by on Church Street. "I'll probably help with the investigation. I'd like to know what happened to him."

"How do you plan to do that?" Sam asked.

"I'll ask to work the case with the ME's office." She shrugged. "I'll try not to put anything extra on you and Selena."

"Don't worry about us," Sam said. "We can handle it, especially now that Tucker is out on his own."

She smiled at him. "And you're happy with his work?"

"Fat chance," Selena muttered under her breath.

"I'm sure he'll be great." Sam darted an evil look in Selena's direction. "Anyway, Peggy, if you need any help, let me know."

"Hey!" Emil yelled from the front of the shop. "Anybody here looking for food and drink?"

"At last!" Walter pushed to his feet. "I thought I might die of thirst."

Sam helped Peggy to her feet, nodding at Walter's retreating back. "Kind of an odd choice of companion to have along on a murder investigation, isn't he?"

"I didn't realize it was going to be an active investigation. Otherwise, I'm sure I would've called *you*."

"Aw, thanks. Nothing I enjoy better than a good murder investigation." He laughed. "Where's Steve? It seems like this would be right up his alley."

"He has his own work—they're looking for some burglary suspects. One dead man isn't very interesting to the FBI."

They walked through the shop together, following Walter and Selena. Emil and Sofia had come from the coffee shop with their order. They were sorting through the cups, and sandwiches in wrappers, at the counter.

"Oh! There she is!" Sofia Balducci raised her hands and eyes toward heaven. "Thank God you're safe! What were you doing out there at that terrible place?"

Peggy thanked her for the cup of hot peach tea. "Terrible place? Are you talking about the motel? Was it on TV?"

"Was it on TV?" Sofia spat on the floor. "Aren't there always vultures where the dead are?"

"*Eww*," Selena whispered, close to Peggy. "I'm not cleaning *that* up."

"We saw you on the TV just a few minutes ago," Emil said. "You were walking out of that place with that big cop friend of yours. You know—he's been here before."

"You mean Al." She took a small bag of almond cookies from Sofia. Peggy always marveled at how the woman could work with such huge rings on her fingers.

"Whoever he is." Emil's thick, dark mustache drooped on the right side when he wasn't smiling, which wasn't very often. Normally he was happy with his life. He prided himself on being a ladies' man with his broad Italian features, craggy brows, and shadowed eyes.

"Al isn't only a police detective," Peggy reminded him. "I've known him for many years. He's my friend."

Sofia grabbed the large cross that was around her neck, and held it in front of her. Her long, black hair fell on either shoulder. "God save us from such friends. Did he arrest you? Were you questioned? I hope there was no sexual perversion involved."

Walter, who wasn't used to the Balduccis, almost choked on his tea.

"There was nothing sexual," Peggy corrected her,

trying not to laugh. "And he didn't arrest me. I'm helping him with a murder."

Sofia put her arms around Peggy and pressed Peggy's face to her ample bosom. "How many times do you have to do these things before your man finds a real job and takes you away from all of this?"

Peggy knew Sofia and Emil's concern was real, if misplaced. They meant well. They didn't understand that Steve worked for the FBI, and that Peggy wanted to run The Potting Shed. They had some odd notion that Steve was some kind of con artist.

"This is the best egg croissant I've ever had," Sam intervened. "What's the secret?"

Emil stared at him. "You take the eggs, and you put them on the bread. No secret."

Selena took up Sam's cause. "And the coffee. What can you say about the coffee except *yum*? How do you do it?"

Sofia and Emil exchanged looks of exasperation.

"Sometimes, it seems you are all crazy." Sofia twirled her finger around her ear so there could be no question of her meaning.

"We have to get back now," Emil said. "You need our help, Peggy, you know where we are."

The couple left The Potting Shed with their heads shaking, bodies leaning together as they tried to make sense of it all.

After they were gone, Sam and Selena burst out laughing.

Peggy shook her head. "You shouldn't make fun of them. They don't understand our culture."

"They've been living here since before I was born," Selena whispered as though the couple was still within earshot. "If they don't get it by now, they never will."

"She's right for once," Sam agreed. "It's not the culture, Peggy. The two of them are wacky."

Walter sighed. "I'm afraid I have to agree with these two. I don't know how you even became friends with them."

"They're very good people," Peggy defended her friends. "They'd do anything for me."

"They make good coffee and sandwiches." Selena smiled. "I guess that's something."

Sam wolfed down his food and coffee. "That's better. Thanks, Peggy. I'm gonna run out to the site to see how Tucker's doing."

"Here we go." Selena finished her coffee. "We'll be lucky if we still have Tucker working for us by the end of the day."

"Why are you so obnoxious?" Sam asked her.

"Because it's fun." Selena grinned up into his handsome face.

"Fun?" He grabbed her and threw her across his shoulder. "Let's see how fun a roll in the manure will be."

Selena obliged by screaming and kicking at him. Eventually, they were barely audible in the back of the shop.

"How do you get anything done around here?" Walter carefully placed his empty cup and sandwich wrapper in the trash. "I couldn't work with that type of shenanigans going on all the time."

Peggy grabbed a paper towel and sprayed it with Lysol before she cleaned up the spot where Sofia had spit on the wood floor. "They're good workers. They're a little high-spirited, but I love them both."

"You must to put up with them." He rubbed his hands together. "Now, on to the bulbs."

Because the bulbs were for fall planting, there was a huge variety. There were Stargazer lilies and Muscadet, which was a fun lily with white blossoms and pink spots.

There was also the Amaryllis Bella Donna which could be planted outdoors even during the summer. The new windflowers, also known as anemones, would be popular. Many gardeners still looked at them as being a protection against evil.

"What is this one?" Walter asked. "It's a little unique."

"They call it the voodoo lily. *Arum Cornutum*. It's lovely. A real showpiece."

"Ah! The hardy cyclamen. These are wonderful in pots," Walter raved.

"I like these Peruvian daffodils too." Peggy picked up some of the bulbs. "They call them spider flowers because of their unique petals. They smell good too."

They finally reached the burlap bags filled with crocus bulbs.

"Which of the new ones do you like?" Walter glanced at Peggy.

"I like the Prins Claus variety. The petals are very white with a deep purple mark on the outsides that looks like someone painted it on them. I also like the Tuscan crocus. It's native to Northern Italy. I got a large amount of them for Sofia and Emil."

"I believe I'd rather avoid something you thought those two would enjoy."

She smiled. "Okay. What about the Cream Beauty? They're one of the first ones up. They're very delicate, maybe like you, Walter."

At first it seemed he might take offense at that, but he finally smiled and took two of the bulbs. "Yes. I suppose I do have delicate sensibilities. Nothing wrong with that. We could all use a little delicacy in our lives."

"Let me get you a bag for those."

Walter left with ten crocus bulbs—and two spider flowers. He thanked Peggy for the adventure, and went out to his Bentley.

Peggy spent some time tidying the shop. It was amazing how things managed to move from one place to another each day. She dusted and hung up the new fall bulbs promotion sign. Traffic was light from the courtyard since it was still before lunch. She knew customers who received the shop's newsletter each month would be in to check out the bulbs that day.

She'd been lucky with The Potting Shed. Charlotteans were avid gardeners all year. Traffic was fairly steady in the cold winter or the hot summer.

When everything was done, she sat by the pond where young cattails were growing. Ponds, and everything that went with them, were big business for the shop. There were large ponds for people with land to put them on and small ponds for balconies and indoor areas. Water plants had become a good sales item for them.

"Sam's almost finished." Selena walked up from the back. "He's lucky I don't take karate lessons or something."

"You pick on him too much." Peggy got to her feet. "One of these days, he's *really* going to throw you in some manure."

Selena laughed. "He better be able to take the consequences if he does."

Sam ignored her jibe as he joined them. "Where are we off to today?"

Magnolia
There are about 80 different species of magnolia that are native to the eastern U.S. and Southeast Asia. Hundreds of hybrids have been created by breeders because they are easy to grow and care for. Most have large, showy flowers and attractive, shiny leaves. Their beautiful flowers are pollinated by beetles, not bees.

Chapter Seven

"How come I never get to go on any of your adventures?" Selena pouted. "You take Sam with you places. You even took Mr. Bellows. I suppose next you'll take Sofia."

"It's because I count on you being here." Peggy smiled. "I appreciate what you do for me."

"Yeah. Thanks. But next time there's an adventure, I want to go."

"Okay. But you might not like it."

"Then I won't go again." Selena stuck her tongue out at Sam. "Try to keep her out of jail, huh? I have tests to study for later."

"You got it," Sam said.

They left for the mini-storage, after Peggy advised Selena about a few things that needed to be done in the shop.

Peggy explained to Sam about what had happened to Harry, and why it was crucial that they go to the auction at the mini-storage that morning.

He was skeptical. "How do you find these people?"

"It was Nightflyer."

"Of course it was." Sam nodded. "What did Steve have to say about it?"

"Not much." She left out the part about almost being arrested. She didn't want Sam to have misgivings about going with her.

He laughed as he stopped at a traffic light. "Only if you didn't tell him about Nightflyer. Does Steve know you're going to the auction?"

"Yes. He knows I need those files. I wish there'd been time for Harry and me to work together, bless his soul." Peggy shook her head. "He didn't deserve to die that way. I hope to get to the ME's office later today, and that they'll let me work on the case."

"If it's poison, won't they give you a call? You're their resident poison specialist."

"I'd like to think so, but you never know. They could bring in the state forensic botanist. I told Al what I thought. I'm sure he'll give that message to Dorothy. We'll see."

Traffic got heavier as they got closer to the storage facility. Peggy wondered where all the cars were going. It wasn't lunchtime yet.

She got her answer as they came to a spot in the road where one lane was blocked. City crews were cutting down a huge, old magnolia tree. The base of it was at least five feet across. There were hundreds of branches that sported the distinctive waxy green leaves and beautiful white flowers.

"What a shame." She mourned the old tree.

"It was getting too big to be at the edge of the street," Sam observed. "It was probably starting to block drivers from seeing ahead."

"I blame the people for that. They should have kept it

trimmed before it came to this. At the rate they're cutting trees in Charlotte, there won't be any big ones left in a few years. We'll look a little strange being 'The City of Trees' without any trees."

"True." Sam nodded thoughtfully, his blue gaze intense. "You know, I've been thinking we should consider adding tree work to our list of services. I've had people ask about it a few times."

They passed the growing pile of branches that littered the street and sidewalk. Peggy guessed that the tree was probably older than the brick house built behind it. There were also some wonderful old oaks in the yard. She hoped they wouldn't suffer the same fate.

"There's a heavy outlay of capital to get started with tree work," she said. "A lot of equipment."

"Yeah. Just thinking out loud." He smiled at her.

"That's what makes you such a great partner! You're always thinking ahead."

"Thanks. You too. I don't regret leaving school to work with you."

"How about your parents? Are they coming around?" Sam's mother and father had been very angry about him becoming a landscaper instead of a surgeon.

"They still aren't happy about it, but we're okay. It helps that Hunter stuck it out and became a lawyer. At least they can point to *her* with pride."

Hunter was Sam's only sister. She'd managed to find a legal firm that took her on so she didn't have to forage for work. Peggy knew Sam was still smarting from his parents' rejection of his new occupation. He didn't like to talk about it.

"I'm sure it's not that bad."

"I guess it all depends which side you're on."

She decided to change the subject and asked him about getting rid of the English ivy on her roof.

"The best way is Roundup," he joked. "But if you

don't want to kill off every other living thing in the area, have them use apple cider vinegar. It'll take more than one application, but it will get the job done."

"Thanks!" She texted Dalton as Sam told her. "I'm sure that will do it."

"No problem. That's my job."

"There it is." Peggy pointed to the large sign for the storage facility. "I hope the gate is open. I'd like to get my car out without a lot of fuss."

"I can always create diversion, and you can sneak it out," he offered.

"Thanks. Another great reason I love having you as my partner—you're sneaky!"

But it was as she'd originally thought—the gate was open—welcoming bidders to the auction of several storage units. Sam parked the truck at the entrance, and they walked to the office.

A dozen or so people were lined up to bid on the contents of those units. Peggy signed in with her name, address, and phone number. She hoped the manager wouldn't pay close attention to her. He was the same man who'd wanted to press charges against her. She stood on the other side of Sam, just in case.

He came up to them and shook Sam's hand. "Welcome. We have six units up for bid today. No promises what's inside them. It could be trash. It could be treasure."

"Sounds like fun," Sam said.

The manager grinned. "I should charge just for the *fun* of doing it. There have been many treasures found here in the past. Usually bidders pay a pittance compared to what they find inside."

"Excellent." Sam glanced at Peggy hugging his side, her nose buried in a sales flyer. "Thanks."

After the manager had left them, Sam whispered to her, "Did you know you have to get the buy the whole unit?"

"No, but that's okay. I brought my checkbook."

"I'm glad I didn't bring mine. I'm a sucker for this stuff."

She moved with him as he started walking. "Do you want to tell me why you're hiding behind me?" he asked.

"No. Not really." She frowned, feeling she owed him the truth since he was there with her. "The manager and I had a little run-in last night when I was here with Harry. Nothing serious."

Sam shrugged, turning so that Peggy was behind him again as the manager walked by to welcome another bidder. "It's your show. We'll do it your way."

She smiled. "Thanks."

Harry's unit was second on the list of those being auctioned. The group walked with the manager to the first storage unit. The auctioneer said most of the items listed in the unit were furniture.

"What is my bid on this first unit?" the auctioneer asked. "Do I hear one hundred dollars?"

"I'll bid fifty dollars," a tall man in a red T-shirt said.

"Fifty dollars." The auctioneer glanced at the manager. "Do I hear fifty-five dollars? Come on, folks. There could be some valuable furniture inside. Do I hear fifty-five dollars?"

The unit finally went for seventy-five dollars. When the door was opened, it was filled with old furniture. Peggy recognized many of the pieces as valuable antiques. They would probably sell for a lot more at an antique auction. "He got a good deal."

"I'll say!" Sam agreed. "See something you want?"

"No. We have more than enough old furniture."

As the small group was leaving to go to the next unit, an older woman walked up and demanded that the proceedings cease. "This is *my* furniture." Her voice trembled. "I have the money to pay the back rent now. You have no right to sell it."

The manager shrugged. "I'm sorry. You had plenty of advance notice that this was going to happen. We've sold it all. You could probably buy it back from this gentleman."

The woman had a look of horror on her face. "No! These things have been in my family for generations. They're priceless. They can't be gone."

"I am within my legal rights to sell everything in this unit," the manager said with a touch of disdain. "Check your contract."

Peggy felt sorry for her. She couldn't imagine if someone had put all of *her* things up for sale without her consent. Even if the woman knew it would happen, it rankled. It wasn't a good practice, but what else could the storage facilities do with items that no one wanted? They probably couldn't afford to keep storing them.

She watched as the woman sobbed when a beautiful rosewood desk was taken to a truck that held other pieces of her furniture. There was nothing Peggy could do to help. It was doubtful that the woman had enough money to buy back her belongings since her lease hadn't been paid in months.

"Okay folks." The manager drew the group away from the grieving woman. "We're moving on to the next unit. Come this way."

Unit 34 was around the corner and down the lane. Peggy's imagination wandered through all the other storage units as they passed. There could be anything inside the large and small units. Jewelry, clothes, shoes, household items. Harry had told her that he'd seen a man pull a forty-year old Mustang into one of the big units. What secrets could these cubbies hold?

The manager waited for everyone to catch up before the auctioneer got in place with his battery-powered microphone and clipboard.

A man standing beside Peggy was having a hard time breathing. He was a large man, way over six feet, with broad shoulders and chest. Despite the heat of the day, he was wearing a brown corduroy jacket. She listened to him wheezing before he brought out an inhaler and took a deep puff.

Was this the same man who'd walked passed her when she and Harry were there?

With a careful hand, she pretended to take a picture of the storage unit, but she had the camera on her phone faced toward her, instead of away. She turned it slightly to the side where he was standing and snapped a photo of the man's face. It wasn't very clear, but it might be enough to identify him.

Maybe she was wrong. He might not be the man who'd passed her. Or he had some legitimate reason to be out there. In either case, no harm done. He didn't know she'd taken his picture.

Harry had told her that he thought people were following him. He thought it had been to get the files he had stored in this unit. Now that he was dead—probably murdered—his words didn't sound so much like fantasy. But it seemed to her that it had been a mistake to kill him without securing whatever was inside.

Unless the killer was there with them now.

She surreptitiously stared at the other people waiting for the next auction. There were at least a dozen men and women. Any one of them could be Harry's killer. She kept a close eye on the wheezing man.

"What are my bids on this unit?" the auctioneer asked.

"Five hundred dollars." The wheezing man raised his hand first.

The manager smiled.

Peggy could tell that must be a great first bid, especially compared with the first unit. It could only go up from there.

"Five hundred dollars," the auctioneer called. "Do I hear five-fifty?"

Peggy raised her hand. "Six hundred."

The auctioneer pointed his gavel at her. "Six hundred. Thank you. Do I hear six-fifty?"

"Eight hundred." The wheezing man seemed determined to have the unit. He glared at Peggy and stepped in front of her.

"Nine hundred." Peggy ignored him and bid again. She was glad the others in the group weren't bidding too. Maybe it was too rich for their blood.

"One *thousand*!" The wheezing man called out before the auctioneer could repeat Peggy's bid, or ask for another.

Sam folded his muscular arms across his wide chest. "Seriously?" he whispered to her. "How high are you prepared to go with this?"

"Eleven-hundred," Peggy called out with a lift of her chin, letting the wheezing man know that she wasn't backing down.

"Fifteen-hundred," the wheezing man said loudly.

The rest of the group was starting to mutter, waiting for the next bid. The manager was rubbing his hands together. Suddenly, auctioning this unit was exciting.

"Sixteen-hundred." Peggy held up her hand.

"Seventeen-hundred," came the wheezing man's bid.

She hoped the smaller bid meant he was running out of money. She was only prepared to go to two-thousand dollars.

"Seventeen-fifty." She flashed a cheeky grin at him.

"Twenty-five-hundred dollars." His flinty eyes dared her to bid any higher.

Peggy wished she could shove that dare in his face, but she couldn't go any higher. When the auctioneer pointed his gavel at her, she shook her head.

"Twenty-five-hundred, going once." The auctioneer paused, and stared at the crowd—especially Peggy. "Going twice? Sold to the man in the brown coat."

Bamboo
Giant bamboos are the largest members of the grass family. Bamboo is also one of the fastest-growing plants in the world, with a unique rhizome-dependent system. High quality bamboo is said to be stronger than steel. The plants make wonderful fences, and deer don't like to eat them!

Chapter Eight

Peggy didn't like to lose.

She ignored the smug look the wheezing man gave her. She'd done the best she could to secure Harry's files. She'd hoped the wheezing man might open the unit after he won the bid, but instead, he went with the manager to pay for what he had and probably pick up the key. She wouldn't get to see inside, as she had the unit with the furniture.

"Sorry." Sam studied the wheezing man as he walked away with the manager. "What could be so valuable in there that he'd be willing to pay so much?"

"Maybe the same thing I'm looking for—only he wants to keep those files away from anyone searching for the truth."

Sam shrugged. "Or maybe he's looking for some *different* truth. What's in there, Peggy?"

She explained about John's files. "I don't know if any of it is true, but I really wanted to find out. I need to get my car out of here before they auction it too."

"How are you going to do that?" Sam walked with her down the twists and turns between Unit 34 and her car.

Peggy hadn't realized how far she'd walked last night, probably because she'd been so intent on finding Harry.

"Just drive it out, I guess." Her tone was bitter. It was over. She might never know if what Harry had said about John's death was true. It was disappointing, though there was nothing she could do about it, even if John *had* been killed because he was working with the FBI. John would still be dead. It wouldn't bring him back.

The truth about it seemed precious to her. She couldn't explain it rationally. It had obsessed her since she'd first heard it.

"Wow! Look at that!" Sam exclaimed as they passed a huge stand of dark green bamboo that had been planted as a buffer between the storage buildings and the main road. "This is the native bamboo I'm encouraging to grow at Sandra Mansfield's house. It's probably been here for ten years, at least, to be so thick. It must be twenty-feet tall!"

"It can't be cut down either since the state declared it an endangered species," she said. "It's beautiful." She touched the tall, sturdy shoots, grateful for the distraction.

"What are you hoping to gain by doing this anyway, Peggy?" Sam put his hand on her shoulder. "You already *know* John was murdered. What good would files detailing the whole thing be?"

"They might not be any good at all," she admitted. "Harry said he had some information pertaining to why John was killed and that it wasn't simply a random act. I don't know."

"He seems like he was kind of a shady character. Not really surprising, since Nightflyer set the two of you up."

Peggy glanced up at him impatiently.

"What?" Sam grinned at her. "Come on. I don't have to be a brain surgeon to see that Nightflyer is a little on the corrupt side. I'm *sure* you know it too. How many times has he gotten you into trouble?"

"He knows things, Sam—things the rest of us don't know." She started walking toward her car again.

"Well, if he knows that John's death wasn't what it seemed, why doesn't he just come out and tell you? Why all these games?"

"I don't think Nightflyer knows *exactly* what happened to John." She defended her online friend. "He set me up with Harry because Harry was part of what happened. There's also the question about what happened to Harry's wife."

Peggy used her keyless entry to open her car. Sam held the door open for her as she got inside.

"All I'm saying is that I don't think Nightflyer is the best place to get information. I'm sure Steve told you the same thing."

"And I expect *that* kind of thing from Steve. I wasn't expecting it from *you*."

He nodded. "Sorry. I wanted to say it before anything else bad happens. I love you, Peggy. You're like a second mother to me—besides being the only one crazy enough to let me help them run their garden business. I don't want anything to happen to you."

Peggy smiled, tears starting to her eyes. "I love you too, Sam. But I have to do what I can to find out what happened to John that night. He would've done the same for me."

"I know. I'll meet you back at The Potting Shed later. Just be careful, huh?"

"I will."

She watched him disappear between the storage units as he headed back to the parking lot by the gate to get the truck. He was such a dear man. She was lucky to have him working with her.

But she still lost the contents of Unit 34. What was she going to do about *that*?

All those uncomfortable conversations with Harry were for nothing if she didn't find a way to see what was inside the unit. She looked at the wheezing man's picture on her phone. This was one thing she had that no one else did. With any luck, she could run it through the police database and find out who he was.

It suddenly struck her that she could find out *exactly* who he was and where he lived. All she had to do was get a look at the names and addresses on the sign-in sheet at the office. There weren't that many people. She could look them up quickly until she found him.

She pulled the car through the passageways between the buildings until she reached the office. The wheezing man was shaking hands with the grinning manager before they parted ways. The manager walked briskly back into the storage unit maze. The wheezing man got into a white, older model Cadillac and drove away.

Peggy scavenged for a pen and paper to write down the license plate number. *South Carolina CHS1212.* She waited a little longer to make sure they were both gone before she parked her car and went into the office.

She was prepared to come up with a story for whoever might be inside. No one was there. The paper with all the names and addresses was still on the desk. Peggy used her cell phone to take a picture of it. If she helped the police with the investigation into Harry's death, she could coordinate the information on the paper with the license number.

She left the clipboard and sign-in sheet on the desk, and glanced carefully outside before she stepped out the door. She was getting into her car again when the manager spotted her. This time he recognized her and started running toward the office.

"Hey you! What were you doing in there? You'd better not come back here again. I'll call the police."

Heart pounding, Peggy left the storage facility as quickly as she could. At least she got some information, even though she didn't get the files. Her breathing slowed to normal once she didn't hear any sirens or see any police cars following her.

"Now, Mr. Wheezing Man." She looked at his picture on her phone when she stopped for a red light. "Let's see who you really are!"

Firebush
Also known as the hummingbird bush because the little birds can't get enough of it. The red bush hails from Central, South, and North America. Firebush is known for its herbal properties since the small black berries are edible, and a salve is created from the crushed leaves to aid healing in skin lesions.

Chapter Nine

Once on the main road, Peggy pulled off at a convenience store, and took out her phone again. She gave Dr. Dorothy Beck, the medical examiner, a call.

"Peggy! I was wondering when I'd hear from you."

"You could've called me," Peggy said. "Did you get my message about Harry's Fletcher's death?"

"I did. I suppose you'd like to work with us on that?"

"I would. I'm fairly certain he was poisoned. It might not be botanical. It occurs to me that it could be a crime of opportunity."

"And that would mean?"

"Maybe some chemical the killer found at the motel room, probably under the bathroom sink."

"Well, since you put it that way, please join us. If it's not a botanical poison and you don't want to stay, I'll understand."

Peggy smiled. "Thanks, Dorothy. I'll be there in a few minutes."

At least that went well. Peggy started the car and drove

toward the morgue and medical examiner's office. Being part of the ME's investigation would open some doors for her that she couldn't open by herself. It would also mean computer access into the police database.

She knew Nightflyer might also be able to help her in finding Harry's killer, but he was unreliable. It could be days before she heard back from him. She disagreed with Sam that he wasn't trustworthy—he was outside the law, which made it difficult for him. Peggy believed Nightflyer was sincerely trying to help her.

She got a call on the way across town. It was Paul. Her heart started beating faster when she thought Mai could have actually gone into labor.

"Mom?" Paul began. "I want to ask you about something I heard today."

Mai wasn't about to have the baby. "What's that?"

"I heard you were picked up last night and accused of breaking and entering. I also heard that you're looking into Dad's death. Was he really involved with the FBI? Why didn't you tell me what was going on?"

There was an undertone of anger and hurt in his voice. Peggy didn't want to make it worse. Honestly, police stations were as bad as beauty salons for gossip.

"I haven't found any *real* answers," she told him carefully. "If I'd really learned something important, I would've told you. You know that. Right now, I'm just chasing ghosts."

"Was the dead man you found this morning involved? Who was he?"

Peggy really didn't want to answer his questions, but she knew she'd have to say something. Better to do it in person, she reasoned. It would make them both feel better.

"Traffic is bad out here, Paul. Maybe we could meet for lunch and talk about this. I'm going to be at the morgue.

All those food trucks are out there around noon. Maybe we could eat and talk."

"I'll be there," he promised.

"Okay. I'll see you later."

The phone call ended abruptly. She was only left with her son's picture on the screen. He was already upset.

Paul reminded her so much of John, even though he had her bright red hair, spring green eyes, and her temper. He had John's nose and his smile. When he talked, it was like listening to John again. He had similar mannerisms to his father too. She thought of him as a nice pairing of everything good she and John had to offer.

Paul had held on to his personal theory that his father's death was something more than a domestic violence call gone bad. They'd argued more than once about it. If she'd listened to him sooner, finding the evidence she needed to prove what had really happened might have been easier.

She knew he would welcome this new theory. What boy didn't want his father to be a hero? She wished she wouldn't have to give it to him half-baked. She wasn't sure what he might do. There had been a time when she'd been worried that he might go after the man the police said had killed John.

Peggy realized she had no choice but to tell him what she knew. She hoped he wouldn't do anything foolish because of it. After John had died, Paul was all about vengeance and finding his father's killer. That had gone away in time—although it had been enough to change Paul's ambitions. He'd dropped out of school, where he'd been studying to be an architect, and joined the police academy.

She knew her son's emotions ran deep—especially on this subject. Hers did too. It was too bad that Harry had danced around the answers until it was too late.

She parked in the morgue parking lot, picked up her bag, and locked the car. The morning was turning hazy with the late summer heat. White clouds, mostly ozone, obscured the blue sky. Just walking from the car to the building brought on heavy breathing in the thick, moist air.

It was obvious to her that the bushes decorating the front of the building had been recently pruned. It was also obvious that the person doing the pruning had no experience. The firebushes, azaleas, and holly had been brutally cut down to the dark, red soil. They'd be lucky if they survived the remainder of the summer heat.

A few years back, there had been an uprising at one of the city council meetings over crape myrtle trees being pruned too far. The city had actually reprimanded the maintenance people who'd done it.

Peggy thought they could all be a little more careful with their trimmers. This wasn't like hair. A good pruning helped a plant. A bad one could kill it.

The guard at the front door greeted her as she passed through the metal detector. It had been months since she'd been here, but Tom still remembered her name.

"I'm surprised you remember me." She smiled at him. "You see so many people go in and out each day."

"How could I forget the lady who gave me and my wife our first good trip to the beach? Having my son, Zac, chew on ginger root kept him from being carsick all the way to Myrtle Beach. We tell everyone about it now."

"Thanks. I'm glad the ginger worked so well. How is your son doing?"

"Strong as a horse, like his dad." The guard grinned. "You're clear, Dr. Lee. Thanks again. Have a good day."

She walked down the long hall to the medical examiner's offices and grabbed the white jacket with her nametag on it. She hoped there was some progress on Harry's autopsy. Surely something would go her way that day.

Dorothy called her to her office right away. Peggy said hello to some other workers in the hall. It seemed that everyone remembered her. It was probably silly on her part to think they wouldn't. Sometimes she went months without working here. Crimes suspected to be committed with botanical poisons were rare.

Peggy was actually giving a lecture on that subject in two days. Queens University had asked her to come back from time to time as part of a lecture series. She'd retired from full-time teaching at the school, but she liked to go back for short sessions. It gave her plenty of time to run The Potting Shed and keep up with her own projects—and still draw a paycheck from them.

The university was expecting a large crowd of law enforcement officials for the lecture on poisons that had been linked to murders. They had used her forensic credentials, and her time at the university, liberally.

She'd been hoping to use Ann Fletcher's case for the lecture. A twenty-year-old murder case that had been ruled accidental death, but proven botanical poisoning, would be a hit with the law enforcement crowd. But she didn't have enough information to use it. It seemed unlikely that she ever would, unless Ann's death was somehow linked to Harry's, *and* she could prove it.

"There you are!" Dr. Dorothy Beck got up from behind her crowded desk. She was much taller than Peggy, and gaunt as a scarecrow. "I almost wish there were more cases of poisoning so you could be here all the time. It's always a pleasure working with you."

Her tone made Peggy's sun-pink face turn red. "Thank you. I enjoy working here too. But I don't think a bumper crop of deaths by poison would make anyone happy."

Dorothy laughed as she caught her reading glasses that fell off the end of her nose. Her brown eyes gleamed. "Well, we have you here now. Let's make the best of it."

Peggy walked alongside Dorothy toward the area

where autopsies were performed and bodies kept in cold storage.

"So how is Mai doing? We miss her a lot. She must be due any minute." Dorothy smiled at her.

"Yes. We had a false alarm early this morning. I think she's ready to get this over."

"Aren't we all when that time comes?"

Peggy laughed. "I think so. The body can only take so much stress."

"Thank God I only put myself through that once!" Dorothy said.

"I feel the same way!"

"I understand the victim was a friend of yours." Dorothy put her glasses back on the end of her nose. "We've already been working on him. If you'd rather not go in, I'll understand. I'm sorry for your loss."

Peggy tried to decide if she should tell her the truth. They'd become good friends since Dorothy had moved here to take on the job of chief medical examiner for the city. But she was still part of the system. Peggy didn't want her efforts hampered toward finding the information she wanted about John.

"He wasn't exactly a friend." Peggy decided on a partial truth. "We were working together. He believed his wife was poisoned twenty years ago. I was helping him with that."

Dorothy frowned. "Was he thinking about exhuming the body?"

"I think he was. First we were going to take a look at her autopsy files and see what the report actually said."

"What was listed as cause of death?"

"Harry told me it was listed as accidental death."

"But he had reason to consider it was murder? And murder by poison—as we were just saying—a rare beast."

Dorothy stared down at her. "You know I love a good puzzle. Give me her name. It seems a little coincidental that he may have been poisoned too. Or are you basing your supposition about what happened to him because of his wife?"

"No. I was the one who found him this morning." She explained what he'd looked like. "There was no sign of trauma. I hope they were able to find the bottle the scotch came from."

Dorothy looked at her tablet as they reached the first autopsy room door. "I don't see anything about that here, but we did send in a sample of the liquid the police obtained from a broken glass. Is that accurate?"

"Yes. It wasn't much of a sample. We should probably nudge the police to see if they recovered the bottle."

"We should have something on his stomach contents too. If his death occurred quickly, all the better for us so the poison didn't have time to disperse." Dorothy handed Peggy a facemask and gloves.

"Let's hope that's the case. I wasn't close to Harry Fletcher, but I don't want to let him down either."

"We won't. Not with both of us on the case."

They went through the doors into the autopsy room. A body was on the slab, covered by a green sheet.

This was the part that, for all her objectiveness, was difficult for Peggy to get through. It was much different dissecting a plant than a person. Her six weeks of training to be a forensic botanist hadn't prepared her for the reality of the autopsy room. It wasn't pleasant.

Dorothy consulted her tablet as she moved the sheet from Harry's head and chest. "You're right in thinking there were no trauma marks from any weapons. He wasn't strangled or knocked unconscious. Stomach content is still being examined. What should we be looking for if poison is involved? Any ideas on what type of poison?"

"I'd expect to see the foaming around the mouth, as I

did. There may be some residue around the lips. If the poison is plant-based, it would likely be a glycoside. It would have to be a large amount for him to keel over and die right away. The scotch could certainly have mitigated the taste. If he'd lived for very long, there would've been vomiting and maybe some blood. Nothing like that was at the scene, as far as I could tell."

"Glycoside." Dorothy put that in her tablet. "Any way to know what kind of plant that could be from?"

"No. Not without further analysis," Peggy explained. "Glycoside is a common poison found in many varieties of plant life."

Dorothy pushed her glasses back on her thin face. "Do you think his wife was killed by the same poison?"

"I haven't been able to see his copies of the police and autopsy files." *Another thing Harry kept in his storage unit.*

"What was her name?"

"Ann Fletcher. Sorry. No date of birth or any other helpful information. We'd only just got started when I found him this morning."

"Okay. We can look for her name. You said she died twenty years ago? We'll see what we get from that."

Dorothy put down her tablet, and picked up Harry's left hand. "These were the only marks we found on him."

Peggy looked at the small cuts on his fingers. "He was using that hand to hold the glass. It broke when he fell. I'm surprised there was no blood with the scotch."

"Maybe someone moved him. Or they cleaned up the blood. He was definitely still alive when he was cut."

Dorothy got a call. "That was the lab. They're starting on his tox screen. Maybe that will give us some answers. I guess that's about all we can do for now. Would you like to research his wife's death, or would you like me to assign that to an intern?"

Peggy knew this was her chance to look up the wheezing man as well. "I'd be glad to do it. Thanks."

"I knew you would." Dorothy smiled as she stripped off her gloves and dropped them in the trashcan near the door. "Let me know if you turn up anything interesting."

"I will." Peggy took off her gloves and mask. She glanced back at Harry before she left the room. She hoped she could find the answers that he was willing to risk his life for.

That was the thing they'd shared that it was difficult to put into words. She was willing to risk her life, too, if it meant the truth would come out about John's death. She related to Harry immediately on that level.

Harry's death suggested that there was something more going on about what he was looking into. Perhaps someone *was* trying to cover up Ann Fletcher's death—or even information about John.

Harry's death seemed impulsive. He didn't have anything that wasn't in the storage unit—at least not that he'd shared with her. Why not take the contents of that before killing him? Without documentation, there was nothing.

Peggy sat at the desk they always kept open for her. It was much cleaner and neater than any of the other desks in the office—probably because she rarely used it. She glanced at her watch. There was still twenty minutes to go until she was supposed to meet Paul. She thought she might as well dig in.

* * *

Thirty minutes later, Peggy looked up from her computer, and Paul was standing beside her desk.

"Oh, you're here!" She glanced at her watch. "I'm so sorry. I was caught up trying to find information. You know—the police database isn't as easy to use as it looks on TV."

Paul smiled, almost despite himself. "You have to get

used to it. When you use it as often as I do, there's nothing to it."

She got to her feet and kissed his cheek. "Well, thanks for coming in to get me." She grabbed her bag and hung up her lab coat. "I'm ready."

"Good. I'm starving. I saw a souvlaki truck outside. That sounds good to me."

"Did they have salads?" she asked as they walked down the hall together. She noticed the squeaking sound his leather duty belt made. "You know, some saddle soap would do wonders for that."

"It's new." He grimaced. "It'll break in."

Tom nodded to both of them as they left the building. They walked outside to a rapidly-changing weather picture. The blue sky was gone, replaced by heavy, fast moving clouds. Probably still part of the storm at the coast.

"We better get to that food before the sky opens up on us." Paul looked up. "We can always eat inside."

They got to the souvlaki truck—Steve's Souvlaki—they both laughed about that. Paul got his meal, and Peggy got a salad and iced tea, before they felt the first drops of rain. They dashed back across the parking lot and sat in the building lobby with their food.

"So." Paul opened his sandwich. "How about starting from the beginning on what's been going on, and don't leave anything out."

Kalanchoe
Kalanchoe blossfeldiana is a succulent plant from Madagascar that is a member of the Crassulaceae family. It is related to jade trees and sedum. The species can grow up to a foot tall in its native habitat. It is an ideal houseplant as it requires very little care and has bright, cheerful flowers.

Chapter Ten

Peggy explained about the email from Nightflyer and her subsequent meetings with Harry Fletcher, which culminated in her almost being arrested and finding Harry's dead body at the motel.

Paul shook his head, his vibrant red hair cut military style. "How do you find your way into these things, Mom? I thought once you and Steve were married, you'd slow down getting into trouble."

Peggy took some exception to his condescending tone. She raised one cinnamon-colored brow. "I don't exactly see this as getting into trouble."

"They brought you into the station for B&E and trespassing."

"That was unfortunate, but a side effect of looking for the truth sometimes." She studied his lean, freckled face as he ate. "I know you want these answers too."

"But not from Nightflyer or some crazy private detective. I want them legitimately—through the police or the FBI. I know the case is still open for CMPD, and Steve said the FBI is still looking into it. Why isn't that enough for you?"

She was completely blown away by his criticism and lack of rebellious passion she'd believed he harbored about his father's death. "I thought you'd be one step ahead of me on this. There was a time when you wanted to go out into the streets, guns drawn, to look for your father's killer."

He shrugged. "That was a long time ago. I'm not a kid anymore. I know you were afraid being on the job would make me less responsible with my actions, but it's made me more responsible. I can see where every action really *does* have a reaction. I want Dad's killer too, but I don't want to go to prison for it."

Peggy ate her salad and stared at a picture of the beach on the wall. She didn't know what to say. He was so different about her information than she'd thought he'd be.

Paul put his hand on hers. "Don't get me wrong—I want to see a thorough investigation into what happened. I just don't want either of us to go about it the wrong way. Dad wouldn't either. I'm about to be a father. I want to live to see my baby girl grow up. I want you to be around for that too."

She cleared her throat. "I understand. If it makes you feel any better, I'm working with the medical examiner on Harry's death. We'll see where that takes me."

"It *does* make me feel better." He grinned. "Just don't go off on your own again, huh? We both believe in the system. It'll work for us, if we let it."

Peggy changed the subject, asking about Mai. Paul told her his wife was a miserable mess and that he hoped their daughter would be born soon. The dark circles under his eyes told Peggy their own story of sleepless nights. She wished she could tell him it would be better when the baby arrived—but that was really only the beginning of their new lives.

He glanced at his watch. "I've got to get going. Call me later if you find out anything about Harry Fletcher. I'll see what I can find on my end. We can work together on this, Mom, if we stay *inside* the lines."

She agreed and hugged him before he left. She watched him walk into the parking lot and get in his squad car. She was very proud of him, although surprised and a little disappointed by his attitude about what she was doing.

"Is that your son?" Tom asked.

"Yes. That's Paul." She smiled as she gathered up their trash.

"He looks good in his uniform. I'll bet his Dad is proud of him too."

"Actually, his father was a police detective who was killed on the job. He wanted Paul to be an architect. I don't think he would've been happy to see him in uniform."

Tom frowned. "I'm sorry, Dr. Lee. I didn't know your husband had passed. Was it recent?"

"No. It's been a long time. We still miss him. We've mostly moved on." Peggy smiled as she went back through the metal detector. "But you never really get over it, you know?"

"I know. My father was a firefighter. He was killed in a fire when I was sixteen. It's like I'm still waiting for him to come home—even though I'm grown up and have a son of my own."

Peggy walked around the metal detector and gave Tom a hug. "Yes. That's exactly what it's like."

"See you later."

She walked purposefully back down the long hall. She'd managed to find a woman named Ann Fletcher in the police files right before she went to lunch with Paul. She was sure it was the right woman because Harold Fletcher was listed as her husband.

Harry was right about the police not taking his claim of

Ann's death being murder seriously. The police had decided against the expense of an autopsy—Harry had paid for one. Peggy was still looking for that file when she sat back down at her desk.

"Peggy!" One of the young interns she knew stopped at her desk. "I have this plant someone gave me that isn't doing well. I don't know if it's the office or what. Could you take a look at it?"

"Sure."

The intern put a small kalanchoe plant on her desk. "Thanks."

Peggy knew what the problem was. The light from the windows was filtered, and the overhead florescent lights weren't bright enough for the plant to survive. It was wilted and turning brown.

"It's a bit overwatered," she said. "And the light is bad in here. You should probably take it home. There are plenty of plants that would thrive in this environment. You could trade it for one of those."

"But I wouldn't know what to get," the intern said. "Any recommendations?"

"A small philodendron would be very good here. I'll write down a few other suggestions. Plants are good in the office—very healthy—as long as they're the right plants."

Peggy wrote down a few ideas on plants the intern could grow there. As she did, she realized how odd it was not to have anything growing on her own desk. But because she was there so seldom, she didn't want to bring in anything just to have it die while she was gone.

"Thanks." The intern smiled. "Would *you* be able to nurse this plant back to health? I'm afraid I'd completely kill it if I took it home."

"I can do that." Peggy smiled. "I'll let you know how it does."

"Great. I'll see about getting one of these other plants. Thanks for your help."

Peggy looked at the sad little plant. It might not make it, but she could at least give it a chance. For her, it was like adopting pets. Sometimes the pets weren't healthy and needed some TLC. She hoped the plant would get better at her house.

Putting aside the plant that stared up at her pitifully, she tackled the database again for Ann Fletcher's autopsy. It was probably done at the hospital since the police hadn't requested it from the morgue. She looked at the hospital where Ann's death was pronounced—Charlotte Medical. There was bound to be information there.

There was nothing she could find electronically. She picked up the phone and called the hospital. The attendant at the hospital morgue there told her that files more than ten years old hadn't been transcribed into an electronic format as yet. He suggested that she should come and get the file.

Peggy was willing to do that. She took the kalanchoe with her when stopped at Dorothy's office to let her know what was going on. Dorothy told her she was still waiting for the tox screen to come back on Harry. It might be tomorrow or the next day before they had specifics.

The rain was coming down heavier as Peggy sprinted for her car. She started the engine and got out into the heavy traffic.

Rain always brought out the worst in people. Everyone was impatient to get where they were going. The roads were slick and dangerous, holding deep puddles of water in some places. Peggy took her time getting to the county hospital. She made sure she had her credentials from the ME's office, grabbed her umbrella, and walked quickly inside.

The attendant she'd spoken to on the phone was a young man who seemed overly worried about losing his job. He made copies of Peggy's driver's license and her medical examiner's pass twice before pronouncing her fit to take a look at Ann Fletcher's autopsy report.

Even then, there was a snag. She asked for copies to take with her. The attendant told her he couldn't make copies of the files.

A little irritated by the young man's manner—even though she understood he was trying to do his job to the best of his ability—she asked to speak to his manager. He shoved back his chair and grumbled before he finally left the office.

Peggy didn't waste any time looking at the files, in case she couldn't take them with her. She skimmed through the beginning of the report and went directly to what was found in Ann Fletcher's tox screen.

"Convallatoxin," she read aloud. "Glycoside. Especially from the lily of the valley."

Lethal lily.

Everything in the autopsy report went along with the idea that Ann had been poisoned. But cause of death was still listed as heart failure, when it all came down to it. Either no one noticed or thought anything of the convallatoxin.

"Hello." An older man in a pale gray suit introduced himself. "I'm Dr. Miles Wyman. I'm in charge of the morgue here. What can I do for you?"

"Dr. Margaret Lee." She held out her hand. "I'm here from the ME's office. I need copies of this file because it hasn't been posted electronically yet."

Dr. Wyman smiled broadly. "I know *you.* I've attended some of your lectures on botanical poisons. Welcome, Dr. Lee. Of course you can have copies. I'm afraid I'll have to charge you for them. It's not me, you understand. It's just policy."

"Of course." She smiled. "How much?"

"A dollar a page." Dr. Wyman turned to the young man who went to get him. "This is my assistant. He'll be happy to help you."

Peggy's jaw dropped at the price. "There are more than a hundred pages in this file, Dr. Wyman. I think that price is a little steep, don't you?"

"Even if I did, there would be nothing I could do about it. I'd like to help you, Dr. Lee, but this is hospital board policy."

"You realize this is part of a murder investigation?"

He shrugged. "As I said, I didn't make the policy."

Peggy lifted her chin, and stared at him. "Then I'd like to speak with someone who made the policy."

Dr. Wyman looked a little less happy to see her. "I assure you, there won't be any change, even if you speak to a member of the board."

"I'll take that chance." She sat down in the uncomfortable green chair by the assistant's desk. "I'll wait."

"Let me see who's available."

Peggy waited for another twenty minutes, not wasting any of that time as she looked through the documents in the file. By that time, another man in a blue suit approached the desk.

"I'm Dr. Emmett Brown. I'm a member of the hospital board. What can I do for you?"

Dr. Brown didn't look excited at all to meet her when she introduced herself and told him about the problem. "You can see where this would easily cost more than a hundred dollars to have copies made. There must be some exception for the ME's office."

"I don't see why the medical examiner's office should warrant an exemption, Dr. Lee. We still have to pay for maintenance on the equipment and toner."

"You could have your assistant scan them in, and send them to my email. Maybe that wouldn't be as costly."

"That's not our policy. Sorry."

He didn't *appear* sorry. He looked smug and self-righteous. "Then I'd like to speak to someone else on the board. There must be someone here with a little common sense who understands the importance of this information on the murder case."

Dr. Brown sniffed. "This can't be part of a murder investigation, or the ME would already have the file."

"Not if the examiner here at the hospital made a mistake in calling this death an accident/heart attack."

"What are you talking about? No one here made that kind of mistake."

"Perhaps your examiner isn't familiar with botanical poisons." She pointed out the toxin listed in Ann Fletcher's blood. "I wouldn't say those are *naturally occurring*, would you? And let's face it—she either ate a large amount of lily of the valley, or someone artificially put their poison into her in a concentrated form."

"Let me see that." Dr. Brown put on his glasses and mumbled as he read the report. "This is unfortunate, Dr. Lee. We had no idea this woman's death was anything other than an accident."

"I understand that. But as you can see now, it was *not* accidental. Her husband was recently killed, possibly in the same manner. It was why he requested, and paid for, this autopsy. Too bad for him that the people who saw it didn't know what they were doing."

Dr. Brown put his glasses away, his heavy face angry. "I can see your point. The hospital will make a copy of this for you, Dr. Lee, at our expense. Sorry for any inconvenience on your part."

"Thank you." Peggy smiled a little. It was nice to win, even something this small.

The hospital morgue assistant quickly made a copy of

Ann Fletcher's file. He put the papers into a new manila folder and handed it to Peggy.

"Thanks for your help."

He nodded and sat back down behind his desk.

She let it go. There was a lesson here, but she wasn't in the mood to teach him what it was. She hoped he'd pick it up on his own.

Peggy put the file inside her bag and opened her umbrella before she ran back into the parking lot again. She unlocked her car door when she reached it, and was ready to open the door, when the van parked beside her opened its door, keeping her from reaching it.

She started to say something, when a second door opened, blocking her way out of the narrow space that had been created. She was trapped. Really angry at the disembarking passengers, she turned to complain, when a large man snatched the folder from her.

"Dr. Lee." The man smiled, showing even white teeth against his heavily tanned face. His black hair was unruly above his gray eyes. "You're not going to need this information, because you're going to lay off this little investigation of yours."

Peggy recognized the man from that morning at the storage auction. She was smart enough to keep her mouth closed on that realization. "Who are you? What do you want?"

"Let's just say I was a good friend of Harry Fletcher's. He wouldn't want someone poking around in his life—or his death. You need to forget about this, and move on to something else. Maybe you should spend more time with your plants in your *shop*."

"Maybe if someone didn't want people poking around in Harry's life and death, they shouldn't have killed him." She faced him defiantly, trembling with anger and fear.

"You've been warned." His attractive face turned feral.

Someone closed the door behind her, and the black

haired man shoved her hard into the side of her car. Peggy's cheek hit the mirror, and she fell to the wet pavement.

The man got back in the van, and the vehicle drove away.

Apricot
Apricots are particular about the soil conditions in which they are grown. An old saying is that an apricot tree won't grow far from its mother. They prefer well-drained soils. Some require pollinizer trees and must be planted in pairs. Apricots are susceptible to diseases such as bacterial canker, spot and crown gall, and fungal diseases. There should be an old saying that relates to the amount of care these trees must be given.

Chapter Eleven

Peggy sat in her car, doors locked and windows up, for a long time. Her cheek throbbed painfully. It had been cut when she'd been pushed against the car. She examined it carefully in the rearview mirror. It wasn't too bad, probably didn't need stitches.

Her clothes were soaking wet. She knew she would probably be bruised from the impact on her leg and arm. Her hands were shaking so badly that she didn't trust herself to drive until she calmed down a little. And she was freezing even though it was at least ninety degrees outside

Possibly worse than her physical injuries was the knowledge that he'd stolen the file from her. There was nothing she could do to prevent it. She felt ridiculous. How could she have let him get away with it?

She could go back inside and request more copies, but would anyone believe she'd been attacked right outside the hospital and had the file stolen? It seemed unlikely to her. She was embarrassed to even ask.

And yet, it showed she was on the right track. She

knew the man who'd attacked her had been at the auction that morning for the same reason she had been. He wanted Harry's files too. She'd been so busy watching the wheezing man that she hadn't paid much attention to anyone else.

She was finally warm again and beginning to feel even worse just sitting there. She'd been terrified when the man had attacked her—he could have shot her as easily as he'd pushed her down.

Now she was mad. She couldn't go back into the hospital, drenched and dirty, with her cheek sliced open. She'd have to go home first and change clothes. She'd take a closer look at the scratch on her face, but it looked like nothing more than a bandage and some antiseptic cream would take care of.

Then she could come back here for another copy of Ann Fletcher's file—and to fill out a report on being attacked in the hospital parking lot.

She started the car, revving the engine a little higher than necessary. It was temper kicking in. The house was only a few minutes from the hospital. She forced herself to go slow again in the bad weather when she really wanted to put her foot down hard on the accelerator.

Getting into an accident won't make this any better.

Shakespeare, of course, was glad to see her. He whined when she used her schoolteacher voice on him to keep him from jumping on her. "I'm just not in the mood to play right now."

Peggy dropped her handbag on a kitchen chair. The door opened behind her, and she panicked, grabbing the first thing she saw—a large spatula Steve used on the grill. She was certain that she looked ridiculous wielding it against another possible attacker, but it was too late. She was confronting Walter as he came in with a big grin on his face.

He stopped smiling as soon as he saw her. "Oh my world! What *happened* to you?"

"I fell down in the parking lot. Go away so I can change clothes."

"Let me help you with that cut on your face. It may need a few stitches."

"Don't be silly. I've done worse to myself working on plants in the yard. Just go away, Walter. Leave me alone." She almost pushed him back out the door. Shakespeare was whining and trying to get her attention. The dog's large body kept getting between her and Walter.

"I came to tell you that my new apricot tree is finally bearing fruit," Walter said as she was trying to get rid of him. "I thought you might like to come for a look-see."

"Maybe later. I'm a little busy right now." She finally got Shakespeare out of the way enough to close the door on Walter and lock it. She took a deep breath, grabbed her handbag, and marched upstairs to her room.

Peggy stripped off her dress and underwear and then climbed into a hot shower. By then she was really starting to feel the impact of the street and the car against her body. Already bruises were forming on her tender flesh. She was going to be sore tomorrow.

She got out of the shower and wrapped her robe around her, trying to stop her teeth from chattering. It was a little shock and some lingering fear. Nothing to worry about. There was some blood on her towel from the cut on her cheek. The bathroom mirror was steamed up so she decided to sit down at her vanity in the bedroom to take a good look.

"Are you taking up cage fighting?" Steve was sitting on the bed.

Peggy almost jumped out of her skin. She put a hand to her face, glad she hadn't had a chance to pick up some stupid utensil to defend herself against this surprise visitor.

"What are you doing here?" She partially covered the wound on her cheek with her hand.

"I live here. What happened?"

"I meant what are you doing here *now*? I thought you were working."

"I come home for lunch when I can." Steve's smile faded as he got to his feet and moved her fingers away from her face. "Did someone at the auction hit you?"

"Of course not. They would've had to go through Sam." She brushed aside his hand and sat down hard on her vanity bench, wincing at the pain in her posterior. Apparently she'd hit the ground harder than she'd thought.

"I'm not going anywhere until you tell me what happened."

"I don't want to talk about it right now." She studied her face in the mirror. The cut might leave a curved scar on her cheek. It looked clean but still a little bloody.

He put his hands on her shoulders and studied her in the mirror. "Let me help you with that. I think we have some butterfly bandages in the cabinet."

Peggy waited impatiently. She felt silly that this had happened to her and horribly weepy. She wanted nothing better than to turn her face into Steve's shoulder and have a good cry. But where would that get her? Steve would be on the phone with Paul, and they'd never want her to do anything but tend her plants again. That wasn't what she wanted.

He came back with the butterfly bandages and turned her slightly to face him. "Tell me. I promise not to judge."

She looked into his concerned brown eyes and tears gathered in hers. "I don't think I can right now. It wasn't life threatening, but maybe a little careless on my part. I was only doing my job."

He put his arms around her. "I don't care what you

were doing. You can tell me anything."

It all poured out of her as he put the bandages on her face. "I should've noticed the van. It was parked too close to the car. I should've realized something wasn't right."

"How could you have possibly realized someone would go to those lengths to scare you off the case?"

"It's not like I didn't know it was serious and that someone else was involved. Harry was murdered. The wheezing man bid more than twenty-five hundred dollars for the contents of his storage unit. Both of those things are suspicious, don't you think?"

"Yes. They're both suspicious. But even a police officer probably wouldn't have seen that attack coming. Did you report it to anyone?"

"Not yet. I was soaking wet, and my cheek was bleeding. I decided to come home first."

"Okay. Now the thing is to call Al and tell him what happened. Have him meet you at the hospital, and get the video footage from the parking lot around the time you were attacked."

"And get another copy of the file." She nodded, green eyes less watery and more determined.

"Exactly." He kissed her gently. "Want me to drive you?"

"No. You're here for lunch. I'll be done in a few minutes."

"I'll see you downstairs."

"Thanks. I love you."

"I love you too."

Peggy got dressed slowly in emerald green pants and a pink and green summer top. She hadn't realized how sore she was until she bent down to put on her shoes. She wasn't looking forward to the near future.

When she was presentable, she went downstairs again. Shakespeare whined at her heels trying to get her to play with him. She patted his big head and told him it was all right. She knew he was just reacting to *her* mood. She tossed his rubber ball down the spiral stairs. He went skidding and sliding to the ground floor, overjoyed at her being happy with him again.

Steve was still in the kitchen finishing his lunch and checking his email on his laptop. "I made you a sandwich to take with you."

"Thanks. I had lunch with Paul." She put it into the fridge.

"Don't forget the video. They might be able to ID the man who attacked you."

"I won't forget." She smiled at him as she put on a clean, dry, rain poncho. "Thank you for not getting upset and demanding to come back out with me."

He kissed her, but his brown eyes revealed the depth of his emotions that he was keeping under control. "You'd better go quickly before that happens. I'll see you later."

* * *

Peggy was feeling rebellious when she returned to the hospital. She'd parked in a no-parking zone close to the door where the morgue was located.

She'd called Al first and let him know what happened. She called Dorothy afterward and explained the situation. Dorothy was upset and offered to find a police escort for Peggy to return to the medical examiner's office.

"I'll be careful," Peggy told her. "I'm meeting the police in a few minutes."

"It looks like your theory about Harry and his wife must be true. Be careful. I don't want to do *your* autopsy."

Peggy saw Al pull into the parking lot as she finished speaking with Dorothy. She met him at his car as he came up behind her.

"You didn't have to prove that Harry Fletcher had a checkered past and enemies." Al put his big arms around her. "We already *knew* that. Are you okay? Do you need a doctor to look at that?"

"What I need is the video footage of the parking lot from about two hours ago when I was attacked. The man who confronted me might be on that tape. He was also at the auction of Harry's papers this morning."

"You've been busy," he said. "Did he buy the files you were looking for?"

"No. But I might have the name and address of the man who did." She told him about their bidding war.

He whistled when he heard how much the wheezing man had paid. "Let's go inside and talk to someone in charge about that video. Twenty-five hundred, you say? Harry *must've* had something important in that storage unit."

Al and Peggy confronted the same young man at the morgue desk. But this time Al sent him scurrying for hospital security when he took out his badge. Dr. Wyman returned with the head of security. Al shook hands with both men and then demanded a copy of Ann Fletcher's autopsy report as well as the video footage.

Dr. Wyman gawked at Peggy. "We just gave you a copy of that report. What kind of game are you playing?"

"She's playing the kind of game where she works for the medical examiner's office, and she was assaulted in your parking lot. The file was stolen from her not even a hundred feet outside your door." Al didn't pull any punches. There was no doubt, looking at his angry face, that he was serious.

"Our security chief will take care of the video footage from the parking lot." Dr. Wyman backed down. "My assistant will get that copy made for you, Detective. I'm sorry about your injuries, Dr. Lee. Do you need to go to the emergency room?"

"No. I just need to get that information back to my boss at the medical examiner's office, thank you."

Al nodded at her as the men went to do his bidding. "How do you think this man knew that you were here getting this file?"

"Maybe he followed me. I saw him at the auction. It wasn't just him, Al. It was at least him and someone else in the van. Each of them opened one of the doors, trapping me there."

"There's a special kind of hell for a man like that who pushes helpless women around."

"I don't consider myself helpless." She smiled. "But they did gang up on me."

"What about this other man who bought Harry's stuff?" Al asked.

"I haven't had a chance to look him up. I'll do that as soon as I get this autopsy report back."

Al shook his head. "You know this puts a different spin on everything, Peggy. I'll go back with you to the ME's office. You give me the information you have about this man, and I'll take it from there."

Peggy didn't like that idea, but didn't have a chance to say so before the security chief returned. He gave Al a DVD of the video from the parking lot and offered to do anything Al needed to clear up the attack.

A minute later, Dr. Wyman and his assistant showed up with the copied files.

"Thanks for your help." Al shook hands with them again. "I'll let you know when we find out what happened."

"I hope you're all right, Dr. Lee." Wyman shook her hand too. "I'll be attending your lecture at Queens. If I can be of any assistance, please let me know."

"Thank you." Peggy smiled, not one to hold a grudge.

She walked out with Al who saw her to her car, and closed the door after her. She knew he was going to follow her back to the ME's office. She was stuck giving him the information he wanted.

Maybe it was for the best. Whatever Harry was into had gotten him killed. Trying to find out what it was had made two men attack her. Maybe it was better for Al to look into it. She could help by working with Dorothy.

It seemed to her as though whatever was going on had to be something Harry had been part of *before* John's death. His wife had died about ten years before John. It may have begun there—a theory that might be proven if they were both killed with convallatoxin.

The rain had stopped again. Watery sunlight followed her from the hospital to the morgue. Dorothy was waiting anxiously when Peggy and Al walked inside.

"Thank heaven you're all right." Dorothy hugged Peggy. "Are you sure you don't need a few stitches in that cut?" She thoroughly examined Peggy's cheek.

"My doctor said it would be all right." Peggy smiled when she thought of Steve putting the bandages on her face. "In the meantime, the autopsy report from the hospital found a large amount of toxin in Ann Fletcher's body. When we get Harry's tox screen back, I think we might find the same thing."

Dorothy nodded. "Would that be reflective of what you saw when you found his body?"

"Yes. It would have to be a large amount of toxin to kill so quickly, but it could be done in food or drink."

"Or scotch." Dorothy smiled.

"Exactly." Peggy took out her phone and sat down at her computer. She removed the micro-SD card from her phone and used it to transfer her photo of the list that she'd taken at the mini- storage to the computer. "I can send this to you, Al. I don't which name is the right one for the wheezing man. I'd planned to go through them until I found him."

"That's great," Al assured her. "I can do the same thing, but faster. I'll let you know when we find something."

Peggy also downloaded the picture she'd taken of the wheezing man. "This isn't a great photo, but it might help ID him." She hoped Al would keep her in the loop on this. "Thanks for your help at the hospital."

Dorothy and Al shook hands before he left. She promised him copies of their results when they came in too.

"So you have Ann Fletcher's file," Dorothy said to Peggy when Al was gone.

"I do. I've already perused it, but I'll go through it more thoroughly."

"Tomorrow." Dorothy put her hand on the manila folder. "I think you've been through enough today. We're still waiting for Harry's information. It will keep overnight."

Peggy agreed with her. "You're right. I have to relieve my assistant at The Potting Shed for a few hours. That's the only trouble with hiring college students—they have tests they have to study for."

Dorothy laughed. "And dates. And countless clubs. Yes, I remember. See you tomorrow. Be good to yourself tonight."

"Thanks. I will."

Peggy walked out to her car, after telling Tom goodbye. She was surprised to find a Charlotte police cruiser waiting for her. The officer told her that Al said to make sure she got where she was going safely.

"Thanks. I appreciate that, but I'm sure it was an isolated incident."

The young man, probably only a few years younger than Paul, nodded and smiled. "This is my job, ma'am. I do what they tell me."

"I know you do. Okay. Let's go."

When she got to her car, she was horrified to see that

someone had sprayed it with red paint.
    Leave it alone!

Blueberry
In Ireland, baskets of blueberries are still offered to a loved one in commemoration of Lammas Day. Once only known as wild berries, botanists have improved the flavor and size of the berries, which we now know are so good for you. These bushes are related to rhododendron and azalea and can be a nice addition to a yard with their white flowers in spring and red-orange fall foliage.

Chapter Twelve

Officer Blandiss was extremely apologetic for not realizing what had happened to her car in the parking lot. He wrote out the report for the vandalism and reported it to Al.

"There was no way for you to know this happened, unless you checked every car in the lot," Peggy told him. "You didn't even know which car was mine."

"Yes, ma'am, but I still feel bad about it since I was sent here to protect you. This paint is still tacky—the vandal may have done it while I was waiting."

"Don't forget it's been raining. It takes longer for paint to dry in this humidity."

Al said he would send a tow truck to bring her car in for processing, in case the vandal left fingerprints. He told Officer Blandiss to take her to The Potting Shed.

"Be sure to thank him for me." Peggy smiled, even though she was shaken at the idea that the people who attacked her were so intent that they would follow her here. She was glad she wasn't in the parking lot again when they were there.

Officer Blandiss nodded. "We're good to go whenever you're ready."

Peggy got into his car, aware of the eyes that were watching from inside the medical examiner's office. Twice in one day was a lot for anyone. It was more than enough for her. She needed to be at The Potting Shed for a while to soothe her nerves. It was difficult to think rationally with so much going on.

Officer Blandiss drove her to Brevard Court but had to drop her off to leave for another call. "I hate to leave you here, ma'am. If you need anything, give Detective McDonald a call. Have a good day."

"Thank you for everything—Luke." She read his nametag. She'd been too upset about her car at the office to notice his first name.

He smiled and gave her a little salute before he switched on his blue and white lights and disappeared into traffic.

Of course, Sofia and Emil were at their street-side window in the Kozy Kettle when she was dropped off. They immediately ran out of their shop to ask what had happened.

Peggy kept it simple, but the cut on her cheek was evidence that there was something more involved than her car being vandalized.

"Oh my good gracious!" Sofia dramatically raised her hands to the sky. "What kind of world do we live in where a man assaults a woman and paints her car?"

Emil shook his head, his thick mustache drooping in the humidity. "Only in this godforsaken place could this happen. America. Land of opportunity to commit crime."

Sofia tapped her long, red fingernail on her cheek. "What about your Aunt Babba? She was thrown down in the street and pulled behind a cart for miles. That was a worse crime than this."

"You're right," he agreed. "But Babba was in her prime—not like poor Peggy here. It might have killed her!"

Peggy had been smiling and trying to sneak away from them as they reminisced about the old days and tried to decide if she was in her dotage. If she could make it inside The Potting Shed, they might not follow. Especially if a new customer went into their shop.

"Oh, look!" Peggy pointed. "I just saw a woman go into the Kozy Kettle."

"Where?" Emil's forehead furrowed. "We should get back."

"Yes!" Sofia took a moment to squeeze Peggy's hand. "I am so sorry. As soon as the new customer is seen to, I'll bring something good over for you. Good food. Good drink. They make us forget the bad things, eh?"

"Thank you so much." Peggy scooted into The Potting Shed.

"What was going on out there?" Selena asked. "I thought I might have to come out and rescue you."

"A police car dropped me off."

"Why did a—*Peggy*! What happened to your face?" Selena's golden eyes were horrified as she stared at the cut on Peggy's cheek.

"It's really not as bad as it looks." Peggy took off her rain poncho. "If you need to leave, I'm here for the rest of the day."

"No way. Not until I hear everything. Quick! Tell me before Sam hears you. I'd like to get the scoop before him for once."

"What scoop are you talking about now?" Sam joined them. The grin on his tanned face disappeared quickly when he saw Peggy. "Are you okay? Do you need to go to the hospital or something? What happened?"

Peggy sat in her old rocker. "I'm glad you're both here together. This way, I only have to say it one more time."

* * *

Sam and Selena sat silently as Peggy outlined the attack and the vandalism on her car.

"It's what you were saying all along," Sam said. "You've got a nose for this stuff."

"In that case, she'd better have some plastic surgery," Selena added. "It's not good for your health to have people beat you up in parking lots."

"It was just a warning," Peggy said.

"A warning that you're going to ignore." Sam was fast to reply. "You should let the police handle this."

"I gave everything to Al. All I'm doing now is looking into the poison that was used in Ann Fletcher's death and if the same poison was used on Harry. That's it."

"Yeah." Selena started to gather her books and backpack. "I'll believe *that* when I see it."

"It's true," Peggy said. "Al has the information from the storage unit. He knows about Ann's death. He's supposed to send me information about the wheezing man who outbid me this morning so I can identify him."

"And then what?" Sam demanded. "Don't go out again by yourself, huh? Not until this is over."

"Sam, I just cut my face. It's not like someone shot me!"

"Not that *you'd* care!" He shook his head. "Have you told Steve?"

"He knows."

"Did you give Al the picture from the auction? Or are you just waiting until Al tells you who the wheezing man is so you can pay him a visit?"

"Even Peggy wouldn't be that crazy." Selena put up her umbrella.

"Don't you know that's bad luck?" Sam demanded.

A wicked grin came over Selena's face. "You mean

opening an umbrella inside like this?" She opened and closed the bright red umbrella several more times.

Sam advanced on her with a murderous expression. Sofia chose that moment to come into the shop with tea and a pastry box for Peggy. Selena almost knocked her down trying to evade Sam.

Sofia stepped quickly out of their path. "You two should take that rough and tumble outside," she barked at them. "There is an old woman in pain here. Be respectful for once. Young people today!"

Selena laughed and waved to Peggy as she left for the day.

Sam offered to get Peggy her cane and shawl so she wouldn't have to leave the rocker and then disappeared into the back of the shop with a hoot of laughter.

Sofia shook herself after she made the sign of the cross on her chest. "I don't know why you have such crazy people working for you. The two of them are like small children. Large, small children. You know what I mean?"

"I know." Peggy smiled when she thought about how crazy Sam and Selena thought Sofia and Emil were. "That's something I love about them. It can be annoying sometimes, but mostly it's good."

"Here is your tea and a nice sweet roll to get you past the bad things. Call us if you need anything. You should not be here alone. Where is that worthless man you call a husband? If this had happened to me, Emil would be searching through the city for this man who attacked me."

"Thanks." Peggy took the tea and white pastry box from her, trying not to take offense at Sofia's description of Steve. "Steve is working, but Sam's in the back."

Sofia waved her hand. "I meant *real* people."

Peggy laughed as Sofia went back across the courtyard to the Kozy Kettle.

No matter what, Sofia and Emil were two of the most good-hearted people she'd ever known. She knew they'd close their shop in a heartbeat and run hers, if she needed them to. She'd do the same for them. She wasn't sure why they disliked Steve so intensely. Maybe he wasn't around enough for them to get to know him.

Peggy had just opened the box that held the delicious-looking sweet roll when the front door bell rang. A woman she recognized from her weekly garden club meetings stepped in. Claire Drummond was a frequent customer who lived in an expensive house, not too from Peggy's. Her husband was a well-known attorney in Charlotte, so she always had plenty of money to spend on her yard.

"I'm so happy you're here, Peggy." Claire smiled when she saw her. She was tall and muscular, her very large, white teeth prominent in her face. "I was hoping to talk to you."

"What can I do for you, Claire?" Peggy put her tea and sweet roll under the counter.

"I'm thinking about clearing all those old holly bushes out of my yard. I'd like to plant beautyberry bushes instead. I just love the blue berries, don't you?"

"I do," Peggy agreed. "But beautyberry isn't native to this area, so it may take more attention than the hollies. I hate to see you rip out native bushes that have probably been in place for at least fifty years."

Claire pouted—not a good look for her. "You sound like my husband. Honestly, what does everyone like about holly bushes anyway? They're prickly, and you said the berries are poisonous, right? I know they're less work, and they made it through the last drought very well. But that's why I have a yard service. I expect *them* to take care of any problems that come up."

Peggy knew Sam had wanted to take over Claire's yard service for a long time. She wished he was up there with them, although she knew he'd feel the same way about taking out the holly bushes.

"I understand. What about something else with blue berries?"

"I don't know. What did you have in mind?"

"What about blueberry bushes? You'd get the same color, and you could eat the berries."

Claire considered it. "I don't know if my yard is right for blueberries, though the idea is intriguing. I've been reading about people planting edible gardens. Maybe something like that would work for me."

"You could have your yard service people test the soil and see if blueberries would live there. After that, you could consider putting in all edible plants. It might even get your yard on TV again. The idea is revolutionary."

"That's exciting, Peggy! That's why I wanted you to be here when I came. You always have the best ideas." Claire's expression turned unhappy. "But I lost my long-time yard service last month, and this new service is only interested in what kind of grass we grow. My husband doesn't care, but frankly, I'd like to rip all the grass out too. What is that but a waste of time and energy?"

No lawn service, huh? Peggy grinned. "You're in luck, Claire. I think Sam could fit you into his schedule."

Claire's brown eyes widened. "Really? You think Sam could—fit me in?"

This was obviously the real reason Claire had come to visit. Peggy was okay with that.

"Let me get him. I know he'll be excited to talk to you about your new project."

"Give me a minute to freshen up," Claire whispered. "Where's your ladies' room?"

Peggy pointed the way and went in back to get Sam.

"Seriously?" he asked, almost as excited as Claire. "She doesn't have a yard service?"

"Not one she's happy with. Although I think she might be more interested in *you* than her yard. I don't think she's checking her makeup for me."

He grinned and tossed back his long blond hair. "Not a problem. I can keep her—and her yard—happy."

Peggy laughed. "It's a good thing all these women don't know you're gay. It might impact the yard service contracts."

"They don't want sex with me anyway," he proclaimed. "They just want someone to pay attention to them. I don't mind sitting around and eating cake after the job is done. That's why they love me."

"You're lucky Selena isn't here now. I don't want to think what she'd have to say to that."

"She's a brat. Where's Claire?"

Sam went back up front with Peggy. Claire shook his hand, her eyes gleaming and lips slightly parted. They decided to take a ride to Claire's house and see if her soil could grow blueberries.

Peggy sat in her chair with a sigh. Her tea was cold, but the sweet roll was delicious.

Customers went in and out, most coming in because they'd received her email about the new bulb shipment. She got a few calls asking her to set some bulbs aside too. She was happy to accommodate customers she knew well with special favors. They were the rock of her business. She couldn't compete with the big box stores around the city—but none of them could match her customer service.

She was surprised to see Al holding the door for a customer who was leaving with a bag of bulbs. When she was alone with him, she smiled. "Are you thinking about something new for your spring garden?"

Al scowled. "You know that I don't know a tulip from a rose. I leave all that stuff to Mary. I have a note from her about some kind of flower bulbs she wants. But mostly I came by to see how you were doing. You had a rough morning."

Peggy took the note from Al and got a bag for his wife's bulbs. "My cheek is a little painful, but not too bad. Did you have a chance to look at my car yet?"

"I looked at it—what a mess. You've really made somebody angry. As far as fingerprints, I won't know about that until tomorrow. Crime scene is all over the motel where Fletcher was killed. The car has to come after that."

"Of course." She put five black tulip bulbs into the brown paper bag. "What about the wheezing man?"

"We're working on that too. So far, no one on that list you gave me has a criminal background. They all seem like good, law-abiding folks."

"Does that mean we don't have pictures of them?"

"That means it's harder to find pictures of them— we're checking with DMV, service records, and that kind of thing. I'll let you know when we have something."

Peggy sighed as she put the last four mixed-color iris bulbs into the bag. "Does it ever seem to you like an investigation takes a long time?"

He thought about it. "No. Not really. It takes what it takes. It's not easy to run down files and people. We're always shorthanded. We could do with a little help, but it has to be help we don't pay for."

She handed him the bag of bulbs. "I could help."

"No, you can't. You already have too much on your plate. Steve might not look real tough, but he'd have my head. How much do I owe you for the bulbs?"

"Nothing. Mary and I will work it out. Sometimes she makes extra casseroles and freezes them for me. That way she has flowers and I have food."

"Don't tell me about it. She cooks all the time." He patted his broad belly. "How am I supposed to pass a physical every year when she always fattens me up like that Hansel kid in the stories?"

Peggy laughed and hugged him. "I'm sure you'll think

of something. Thanks for checking in on me and for the ride over. Officer Blandiss was very polite. I hope tomorrow has better weather so I can ride my bike here."

"Speaking of Steve, you're not gonna make *me* tell him about this, right? He should know what's going on, Peggy."

"You don't have to worry." She waved her hand near her wounded cheek. "Dr. Steve did my face at lunchtime. He knows."

"Good." Al frowned. "Paul was snooping around the Fletcher case a little today. I suppose he knows that you might be looking for new information about John's death too, huh?"

She thought about Paul's calm reaction to her news. "I told him. He didn't seem very interested, unless it was part of a police investigation. Maybe he changed his mind."

"I hope not. He's a good officer, and I'd hate for him to get involved with this goose hunt. Besides, we aren't investigating who killed John. We're looking for who killed Harry Fletcher—and maybe his wife. Let's not forget that."

Peggy agreed. He kissed her forehead carefully. "You need a ride home tonight?"

"No. Sam should be back in time. He can take me home."

"Okay. Watch your back. I'll talk to you later."

Peggy got on the laptop she kept at the shop after Al was gone. Rain had started again, probably keeping any potential customers from paying her a visit until it cleared. She mostly used the laptop to order supplies and check catalogs. She had a large email list of her customers who frequently used that medium to contact her.

Today she thought she might try to get in touch with Nightflyer again. It had been weeks since she'd heard from him. If he didn't already know about Harry, she could inform him. He might have some suggestions on where she could go from here.

But there was no immediate response from her online friend. She knew he'd been on the run for a while, fearing for his life. She had no idea where he was. She knew he had enemies and could only stay in one place for a short time. It made communication very one-sided.

Maybe it was foolish to trust him, but he'd never forced her to follow up on any of his suggestions. That was all her. And his information was sound. It was because he didn't come in and talk to the police—or the FBI—that made Steve, Paul, and Al distrust him.

Rain continued to fall as twilight settled in early. It was only four p.m. but it looked like night. Sam wasn't back yet—though she couldn't imagine him standing outside in this weather talking to Claire about her garden. They'd probably gone inside for that slice of cake he'd talked about. Sam was a good listener and knew more than his fair share of secrets about the women he worked for. Lucky for them, he also knew how to keep his mouth shut.

Peggy decided to call Steve and see if he could pick her up at five.

As she got out her phone, the door opened from the courtyard where the stones ran in deep streams of rain from Latta Arcade to Church Street. A tall, large man wearing a hooded poncho stepped into the shop.

The wheezing man looked up at Peggy, and used his inhaler.

Agastache
*Commonly known as anise hyssop, the coarse leaves of
this plant release their licorice/citrus aroma when they are
crushed. Leaves of this plant are used as a food seasoning
and for making tea. The flowers are edible and delicious.
This is a good plant for the back of your perennial garden
with its tall, upright, blue flower heads.*

Chapter Thirteen

Peggy wished she had something more than a few garden tools to defend herself when she saw him. As he closed the door, she started to dial 911.

"My name is Arnie Houck," the wheezing man introduced himself. "I know you were working with Harry Fletcher before he died."

"Yes." Her heart was beating fast, and her voice sounded slightly strangled. "How did you find me?"

"I saw your sign-in at the auction this morning. I hope you don't mind that I looked you up."

She was ready to push call on her phone, but held off for a moment. He didn't sound threatening. He hadn't actually done anything besides outbidding her. *Maybe* he was at the storage lot when she and Harry were there, but she wasn't even sure of that.

"Why were you looking for me?"

"I wasn't—until I heard about Harry's death—and your name was mentioned. I was hoping you could bring me up to speed on what Harry was doing in Charlotte."

"What do you know about Harry? Why did you bid on the contents of his storage unit?"

"Because Harry was my brother-in-law. He killed my sister."

That statement astounded Peggy. She put the phone down and studied Arnie Houck. He looked to be in his mid to late sixties. His brown hair was thinning above his sallow face. He used his inhaler again, his breathing issues probably affected by the damp weather. He didn't look particularly dangerous.

Was it possible that *Harry* had murdered his wife?

Sam chose that moment to get back from Claire Drummond's house. "She bought the whole deal, Peggy. It will take me months to get everything set up the way she wants it and then start on her yard service maintenance."

He stopped when he saw her visitor. "Hi. I'm Sam Ollson." He stepped forward to shake Arnie's hand.

"Arnie Houck. You were at the auction this morning too."

Sam glanced at Peggy, eyes narrowed as he assessed the situation. "That's right. Anything *we* can do for you?"

Peggy shook her head. "Mr. Houck was explaining to me that he was Harry's brother-in-law."

"Really?" Sam's blue gaze swung to the older man. "I'm sorry for your loss."

Arnie snorted. "Loss? The world is a better place *without* that deadbeat."

"Mr. Houck believes Harry killed his sister," Peggy said.

"I don't mean that in a literal sense," Arnie explained. "The police said my sister's death was an accident, but I'm sure it was brought on by years of worrying about Harry. He was always in and out of trouble. Ann was left to fend for herself more times than I care to think about. Maybe he didn't shoot her with a gun—but Harry was still responsible for her death."

"Why were you willing to spend so much money to get Harry's personal items?" Peggy asked.

"I don't know." Arnie sighed. "I guess I was hoping some of my sister's things would be in there too. I was away when she died. When I got back, he'd cleaned out everything that belonged to her. It was just the two of us, me and Ann. Our parents died when we were very young."

"Have you looked inside the unit yet?" Sam knew how much Peggy wanted Harry's files.

"I haven't had a chance to go through things," Arnie said. "I had some business in town, and then I heard about Harry. You knew he was dead when you were at the auction, didn't you?"

"Yes." Peggy put her hands on the counter. "Harry said he had some information about my husband. He was going to give it to me in exchange for working with him on Ann's death. He believed she was murdered."

"Murdered? That's crazy. I checked with the police when I got here twenty years ago. That was the first thing I thought when I heard she was dead. *They* said her death was an accident."

"There may be some inconsistencies in that theory," Peggy said. "I don't have all the details yet, but the police are taking another look at Ann's death while they investigate Harry's."

Arnie sat down hard on a ladder-back chair that was near the door. "You mean all these years I've accused Harry of killing my sister—and he really *did*?"

"I don't think so. Harry wanted me to help him prove Ann's death wasn't an accident. That hardly seems to be something you'd do if you'd murdered someone."

"If you don't need me up here," Sam said. "I'll be in the back, Peggy."

There was a question in his voice—*are you okay?*

She nodded. "Thanks."

Sam left them, but Peggy knew he wouldn't go far. He'd be listening.

Arnie shook his head. "And you think there's evidence in his storage unit that proves Ann was murdered?"

"I don't know." She was reluctant to tell him anything else until she knew more about him. "Harry claimed he had more information in his papers that he kept there. I wanted to know— so I bid on the unit."

"I'm so sorry. If I'd known, we wouldn't have had to waste that money. We were bidding against each other for the same thing."

Peggy thought about the man in the parking lot who'd attacked her and taken Ann's file. "I'm sorry I made you spend so much money, but if we wouldn't have bid on the unit, someone else might have taken it."

He nodded. "Why do the police think Harry was murdered?"

"It was the manner of his death. I can't say anything more during the investigation."

"And you work with the police?"

"In a way. I work for the medical examiner's office. I'm a forensic botanist. I think Harry was killed with poison."

"Poison?" Arnie scowled. "What kind of person kills someone with poison, especially nowadays?"

"You'd be surprised."

"I guess so."

Peggy wasn't prepared to go into that subject any deeper either. "Did you move everything out of the storage unit?"

"No. Not at all. I'm only staying here a few days. I paid off the past due on the unit and set up an account to keep everything where it is until I can go through it. I'm not sure any of it is worth shipping back home."

"Where's home?" She was elated that Harry's papers were still available.

"I'm from Columbia, South Carolina." Arnie watched her. "Would you like to see what Harry had stored? I could take you down there. We could both get a look at Harry's legacy."

"Yes. I'd still like to see the files Harry was talking about. They could be a big help to the police in investigating his death as well as your sister's."

"Why did he know about your husband's death? Was he involved with that too?"

"He worked on it as a private detective," she briefly explained. "He said there was more information that he'd collected."

"It sounds like him." He shook his head. "Harry wasn't exactly a fan of the police department—*any* police department. His dealings sometimes crossed the line." He used the inhaler again.

"You have more than just asthma, don't you?" she observed.

He nodded. "Emphysema. I was a firefighter for many years. I'm paying the price now."

"I'm sorry."

"Why don't we arrange to meet at the mini-storage? I'll wait for you at the gate, and we can see what's there. You're welcome to whatever you want. If Ann was murdered, I'd like to know too."

"That sounds good." Peggy glanced at her watch. "It's kind of late already, and with the weather—would tomorrow morning work for you?"

"That would work. About nine?"

"All right." She went around the counter and shook his hand. It was cool to the touch. She looked into his slightly yellowed eyes. Arnie Houck was indeed a sick man. "I'm glad you came by."

He smiled. "I have a bad habit of looking over people's shoulders—that's how I saw your name and address as you signed in. It was simple to find you on the Internet. That habit has gotten me into trouble more than once, I'm afraid. Thanks for being so understanding."

"If it makes you feel any better, I took a picture of the sign-in sheet with my phone so I could look up everyone on it as possible suspects in Harry's death."

"I believe you're saying we're *both* sneaky. I'll take that as a positive." He got to his feet, at least a foot taller than Peggy. "I'll see you in the morning."

Peggy watched him walk through the courtyard, hunched over as he was pelted by the hard rain. She should have asked him if he was at the mini-storage last night when she and Harry were there. It didn't seem to matter, but she'd like to know.

Maybe even more important—*where was he when Harry was killed?*

"He's gone, huh?" Sam came up behind her.

"Like you haven't been back there listening the whole time." She accused with a smile, glad that he was there.

"I'm not apologizing for it either. He could've been a bad guy—still could."

"I'll do some research on him tonight. He's probably okay."

"But you think *everyone* is okay." He grinned. "Need a ride home?"

"I don't know. Maybe you're a bad guy. I *am* naïve and trusting," she joked.

"That's true. You could offer to feed me dinner, and then you'd know I wasn't taking you home out of the goodness of my heart. That way, you could trust me."

"Go get the truck while I close up. I don't know who's crazier—you or Selena."

"That's easy. Definitely Selena."

"I'm locking up now."

Peggy gathered her things together, locked up the day's receipts in the safe, and met Sam on the street in front of Brevard Court. "I should tell you that my parents said they might come by for dinner tonight."

Sam put the old truck in gear. "Great! I love your folks, and they always bring good food."

"That's one way of looking at it."

They drove to Peggy's house with Sam talking constantly about the new landscaping contract with Claire Drummond. He was very excited about their plans, and the prospect of another long-term client.

"She has a great piece of property too," he said. "Almost as good as yours. And she loves new plants. She's wants some agastache bushes in her yard."

"If you're hinting that you'd like to work on my property, have at it. I'm sure it could do with a tweak here or there."

"Claire wants a complete makeover."

"Forget that." Peggy smiled at him. "I'm not looking for a whole new yard."

"Just thought I'd mention it. Your yard has been the same way for a long time."

"And it's basically going to stay the same as long as I live there."

When they reached the house, all the outside lights were blazing. Steve was home. Peggy's parents' car was in the drive too.

"I guess we'll be talking about the Shamrock Historical Society over dinner," she observed. Finding artifacts from Charlotte's history was her mother's passion since she'd moved there.

Sam opened his door. "Not if I can get in everything I want to say about my new contract."

"Between the two, we should have some lively

conversation."

Steve had already locked Shakespeare in their bedroom for the evening. His huge, boisterous welcomes were a little too much for Peggy's mother. Lilla and Ranson Hughes, Peggy's mother and father, were gathered around a large pot on the stove. Steve stood off to the side, wearing his red cooking apron that said, *Kiss the Cook.*

"Hello, everyone," Peggy said with a smile. "I knew there would be plenty, so I brought Sam with me."

Peggy's mother gave her a cursory glance at first—until she saw the cut on her daughter's cheek. "What have you been doing to yourself this time?"

Steve shrugged as Peggy's glance went to him. "I didn't say anything."

"It's nothing serious, Mother." Peggy put her handbag on the table. "Just a little accident."

"A little accident where Peggy was attacked because she's looking into someone's death for the ME's office." Sam managed to sneak between the cooks and sniff the sauce that was bubbling in the pan. "Yum."

Peggy's father slapped at Sam's hand as he tried to taste it. "Not hygienic, my boy. Get a spoon if you want a taste."

"You're doing it again, aren't you, Margaret?" Her mother's white-haired head was tipped to one side as she continued to study her daughter's face. "Have you seen a doctor?"

"Remind me never to take your side against Selena again," Peggy warned Sam for his perfidy. Then to her mother, "It looks worse than it is. I'm not worried about it. What's the historical society up to this week?"

It was an obvious ploy to change the subject. Lilla's eyes narrowed. "You aren't getting away from it that easy, my girl."

"The Shamrock Historical Society has a new member." Walter appeared from the hall. "I joined this very day."

"That's wonderful news!" Peggy was still trying to redirect everyone's attention from her. "I didn't know you were interested in history."

Walter's chest puffed out. "History is what makes us who we are! Everyone should be interested in it."

"Ranson and Lilla are making roasted vegetables with cheese sauce." Steve tried to help her out.

"That's right." Peggy's father grinned at her. He took great pride in his small vegetable garden. "I picked them myself this morning."

"It sounds and smells wonderful, Dad." Peggy went around her mother to give her father a hug. "Is that the famous Hughes' cheese sauce I smell?"

He hugged her tightly. "That's right. Grandma Hughes' famous sauce. We should've put it on the market, like the Colonel did with his chicken. We'd be rich by now."

Sam finally found a spoon and got some of the sauce into his mouth. "I agree. What's the secret?"

Ranson laughed. "If I told you, I'd have to kill you. Steve, have you got a gun handy?"

"Always," Steve joked, going to Peggy's side and putting his arm around her.

"It looks like you should've had that gun wherever Peggy was when she got hurt today," Lilla said in a snarky voice.

"I tried to convince her to stay out of it," Steve replied. "You know how stubborn she is."

Walter laughed. "I couldn't believe when I saw her cheek flayed open today. Maybe she needs to take some self-defense courses. I did a few years back. Does wonders for your self-esteem."

Lilla coughed. "My daughter doesn't need any help in *that* department!"

"Has anyone set the table?" Peggy asked in a light voice as though she wasn't irritated by them talking around her like she wasn't there.

"I don't think so," Steve said. "They don't really need me in here. I'll give you a hand."

They went into the large dining room together and started taking out the antique rose china.

"Sorry. I didn't know it was going to be a Peggy-fest tonight." Steve put bowls on the table. "Are you okay?"

"I'm actually better than okay." She glanced toward the kitchen door, but everyone else was involved in making dinner. "The wheezing man came to visit me at the shop."

He stopped with a bowl in mid-air. "And that was a good thing?"

She explained what Arnie had told her. "He might not be who he claims to be, but I figure I can look him up. I might still get a look at Harry's papers."

"I hope you don't plan to go there alone with him tomorrow." Steve put the delicate bowl on the polished surface of the wood. "I can go with you. Or if you're not comfortable with that, call Paul, or take Sam."

"I don't see why Arnie would want to hurt me." She started taking out the crystal glasses.

"But you don't know who the man was who attacked you at the hospital either."

"It wasn't Arnie." Her green eyes were suspicious. "You've been talking to Al, haven't you?"

"Did you expect me not to? I wouldn't have to talk to him—if *you* told me everything."

"I'm telling you everything I know right now."

"Just be careful, Peggy. That's all I ask. You don't know if you can trust this man. For all you know, he could be Harry's killer."

"Men don't use poison," she retorted smartly. "Arnie

seems more like the gun or knife type to me."

Steve gave her an exasperated look, but didn't say anything else about it as dinner was served.

Ranson placed the china tureen on the table between them. "Not good to argue over food. Bad for the digestion."

Paul was able to join them only a few moments after they sat down to eat. His shift had ended early, and Mai was at home asleep.

Lilla frowned. "Oh, that's too bad. I wish she could have come too. How is she doing?"

"I'd rather not talk about it." Paul shook his head.

Ranson slapped his grandson on the back. "Don't worry, son. It only gets worse once the baby is born. This time will seem like a picnic after you live through the next three months."

"Thanks, Grandpa. I might have to take a job out of state if it gets any worse." Paul smiled at Steve. "Got any openings in the FBI somewhere else?"

Everyone laughed at that, and Lilla filled a bowl for Paul. Talk around the table turned to the Shamrock Historical Society's newest project, as Peggy had hoped. The team was excavating an old church cemetery over on Seventh Street.

Once Lilla had started talking about her favorite subject—and Sam had a chance to gush about Claire Drummond's yard—there wasn't enough time to say anything else about what had happened to Peggy. She was grateful to be left out of the conversation.

There was fresh peach pie and coffee for dessert. Mai called, and Paul had to leave. She needed ice cream and a neck massage. He hugged his mother and grandparents and shook hands with Steve, Sam, and Walter.

Everyone helped clean up after dinner, the talk continuing about Charlotte history and gardening. They all walked next door to take a look at Walter's apricot tree. It was beautiful in the odd twilight with the fast-moving storm clouds above them. There were dozens of small fuzzy fruit amidst the pale green leaves.

Peggy walked back to her parents' car with her father's arm around her shoulders. Lilla walked behind them with Steve.

"You know, you have to take care of yourself," her father said.

"I know, Dad. I do."

"You get caught up in things and act impulsively sometimes, Peggy. You've been hurt before."

"I know, Dad."

"You're about to be a grandmother." He stopped walking and smiled at her. "You might have to settle down now."

"I'm not digging up old graveyards." She smiled.

"You've got your plants and your shop."

"Sorry, Dad." She hugged him. "I'm not ready for that rocking chair full-time yet."

"I know." He kissed her lightly on the head. "Just be careful. I don't like to see you hurt."

"I will."

Her mother snatched her father's arm as she came closer. "Time for us to go." She kissed her fingers and tossed the kiss to Peggy. "I don't want to hurt that wound. It looks a little angry. Better have someone take a look at it."

"Thanks for dinner," Steve called out as they got into their car.

"Goodnight," Peggy chimed in.

"You handled that very well." He observed when they were alone.

"Thanks. Now I can go inside and fall apart."

He hugged her close to him. "You're tougher than that."

"Not when it comes to my mother."

Peggy took Shakespeare out for his evening run. The sky was still cloudy, with a few stars trying to peek through. She went in through the basement door when the dog was finished doing his business and chasing anything that moved in the garden. He laid down on one of the rubber mats that covered the concrete floor as Peggy picked up her clipboard to check on her experiments.

She'd collaborated with a group that was trying to erase world hunger by growing bigger, more drought- and insect-resistant, plants. Already they'd come up with wheat and corn that had a shorter growth cycle. She, and her fellow botanists from around the world, kept each other up to date on their projects each week.

Peggy was currently working on watermelons that were packed full of extra vitamins. They had a thirty-day growth cycle from planting to harvest. The fruit was very sweet, and very juicy. It was also small—which many of her associates criticized.

Her answer to that was that people could grow so many of the melons that size didn't matter. She was still working on it, but so far the melons were the size of baseballs.

She had a text on her phone. It made a strange pinging sound in the quiet of the basement.

SORRY FOR YOUR INJURIES TODAY. CLOSE TO ANSWERS ABOUT JOHN'S DEATH. DON'T GIVE UP.

Peggy knew she couldn't text Nightflyer back, but it didn't matter. She was on the right track, no matter what anyone thought. It was only a matter of time before she had more information about what had happened to John.

Lily of the Valley

Convallaria majalis. The lily of the valley is an herbaceous perennial found in temperate areas of the Northern Hemisphere. The dainty white, sweet-smelling lilies bloom in the late spring. The flower is the floral emblem of Yugoslavia and the national flower of Finland. All parts of the plant are extremely poisonous - there are forty different cardiac glycosides in it. Compounds have been made from these poisons since the dawn of history. They were used to treat arrhythmia and congestive heart failure, as well as a sedative. This plant can kill you!

Chapter Fourteen

Al called Peggy as she was getting ready for bed. "I have the name and address of the man who bid against you at the auction today. His name is Arnie Houck. I don't know what his involvement is in all of this."

Peggy debated about telling him that she already understood Arnie's involvement. She finally decided to keep her friend in the loop. "He came by the shop. He's Ann Fletcher's brother."

"Okay. Tell me."

She could imagine Al writing it down in his little notebook with the dull pencil he usually used. "I don't know if he has anything to do with Harry's death. He said he didn't know Harry thought his sister had been murdered."

"Best not to get involved until we know more about him," Al counseled. "We looked through the video from the hospital parking lot. The van doors being open kept us from seeing the face of the man who attacked you. We got the license plate of the van, but it had been stolen. They ditched it over on First Street. Crime scene is checking for prints, but right now we've got nothing."

"Thanks for letting me know," she said. "I'll let you know if I find out anything new."

"From a safe distance, right?"

"Of course. Goodnight, Al."

"Nothing from him, huh?" Steve asked from their bed.

"Not really. I'm hoping to have more answers from the tox screen tomorrow." She smoothed cream on her hands and switched off the light. "I didn't ask you how your burglary investigation went today."

"We didn't have anything as exciting as you did. Just a lot of questions with no answers. Maybe we'll have a better day tomorrow too." He kissed her, and turned over. "Goodnight, Peggy."

"I love you, Steve."

He murmured sleepily, and she closed her eyes.

* * *

The next day was bright and sunny with temperatures promising to be hotter than normal. Peggy and Steve went through their usual morning routines before parting ways to go to opposite parts of the city to work. She had decided to ride her bike to work since the day was nice. It was her normal mode of transportation for the office and the garden shop.

Peggy had an early morning email from Dorothy telling her that Harry's tox screen was in. She didn't say what the findings were. Peggy was eager to get to the office and find out.

If Ann and Harry were killed by plant toxin, it would be unusual. Convallatoxin wasn't a normal poison—poisoners were more likely to use arsenic from rat poison or Drano. She really didn't blame the examiner at the hospital for ignoring, or missing, the findings.

She wondered what the police would make of the deaths being twenty years apart, and yet related so intimately. Poison was a weapon that was mostly used by people who knew you. It wasn't something that usually happened with a stranger.

All of it was speculation on her part. She thought about it as she rode into the parking lot and locked her bike in the rack near the sidewalk.

Tom greeted her at the door, and she passed through the metal detector with a quick step. Peggy went to Dorothy's office first, but the medical examiner wasn't there. She thought to check the autopsy room where she'd seen Harry's body. That's where she found Dorothy.

"Just the forensic botanist I wanted to see." Dorothy's voice was muffled by her surgical mask. "Come in. Wait until you see what I found."

Peggy put on her coat, gloves, and mask. "You said you have Harry's tox screen back."

"I do. There was definitely convallatoxin in his system. I looked at the files you got on his wife yesterday. The big difference was the amount of toxin in Harry Fletcher's system. His wife—someone could look at that, and mistake it for something else. Harry's toxin level was off the charts."

"That sounds like some concentrated toxin," Peggy remarked. "It would be hard to drink enough of that in a glass of scotch."

"I thought the same thing." Dorothy rolled Harry's head to one side. "Look here. A tiny puncture wound. I don't know if we would even have noticed if the notion of poison wouldn't have come up."

Peggy looked closely at the small hole in Harry's neck. "Someone injected him with it. That's why he died so quickly."

"Exactly. I put the time of death only about an hour before you found him." Dorothy was pleased with her find.

"I don't know if we should follow your friend's lead, and request an exhumation order, or not. Ann Fletcher may have been fed the toxin over a period of time."

"Which may be impossible to tell so long after her death."

Dorothy sighed. "True. At least from these files. I really think we should exhume her. We could do tissue samples and still find out how long she'd been ingesting convallatoxin."

"If you think that's the right thing to do. I'm not a big fan of exhumation."

"I think it's best, if we really want to know what happened to this woman."

Peggy was glad they had an answer. Still, convallatoxin wasn't something you could buy at the local drug store. She'd never even heard of someone selling it on the Internet. It seemed to her that someone who'd used it at least twice to kill people would make their own. Certainly, it was too distinctive to think more than one person had used it to kill the couple.

Dorothy got off the phone after ordering the exhumation of Ann Fletcher's body. "Do we know if she has any living relatives now that her husband is dead?"

"Her brother is in town. Will you need his permission?"

"I wouldn't have to get it, but it would take me around a bunch of red tape if I had it."

"I'm meeting him in a short while. I could ask him to sign a permission form." She glanced at her watch. Sam was supposed to pick her up in about twenty minutes.

"Let me get you that form." Dorothy smiled and removed her gloves and mask before she left the autopsy room. "I feel like we're on to something now. Convallatoxin is kind of rare. Someone must be making it.

It seems like an odd choice of ways to kill someone."

Peggy agreed as she removed her gloves and mask to follow Dorothy to her office. "I'll look around and see if I can find someplace local to buy it, but I doubt it. That only leaves the Internet."

Dorothy shrugged. "You can get anything there."

"But this is twenty years apart and basically in the same family. That's a long time to only use one poison, don't you think?"

"You mean they should have changed it up a bit? Who knows what significance it holds for the killer? This could be a crime of passion."

Peggy smiled. "That's a long time to be passionate about something."

"You know what I mean. I'm going to do a search through North Carolina files to see if there have been other convallatoxin poisonings during that time. We might be on to something."

Dorothy gave Peggy a standard exhumation permission form. "Good luck. Where are you meeting the brother anyway?"

Peggy explained about Harry's files. "I may have more to go on by the time I look through them. Harry was so certain his wife was murdered. No one would listen to him."

"It's like anything else that happens when large entities have to deal with it—mistakes can take place. It's unfortunate, but at least he had you to champion him. Honestly, I don't know if any of us would have noticed that tiny needle mark without you pointing us in that direction."

"I guess bullets and knife wounds are easier."

"Anything is easier than poison." Dorothy sat down at her desk, and picked up her phone again. "Let me know what you find out in Mr. Fletcher's files."

Peggy washed her hands in the restroom and gazed at her cheek. It was looking better today, not as red. It really wasn't that bad—definitely not as bad as everyone's reaction to it. She knew her mother hadn't had the last word on it yet.

Sam wasn't in the parking lot when she went outside. Instead, his younger sister, Hunter, was listening to music as she sat in her blue Camaro. She turned her head and grinned at Peggy when she opened the door.

"Hi there. I had some free time this morning so my brother talked me into picking you up to go look for some files." Hunter was a statuesque blond with her brother's blue eyes and a flawless complexion.

"I'm glad you could come." Peggy got in and fastened her seatbelt. "I haven't seen you for a while. How's the new job?"

"Great! I have *money*! It's really nice to have money. I got this car and a new apartment. I have a whole closet full of new shoes and clothes. I even have a new credit card. I love having money again!"

"It sounds like it." Peggy laughed.

"I don't have to ask how you're doing. Sam brought me up to speed. I'm glad too, because otherwise I might have thought Steve took a swing at you." She nodded at the cut on Peggy's cheek.

"It would be more likely that I would take a swing at him," Peggy said. "You know Steve—he's as calm as buttermilk. That's why we're so good together. Having a temper myself, I wouldn't do well spending my life with someone else who had a temper."

"I suppose that's true." Hunter grinned. "That's the only thing I'm missing in my wonderful new life—a man. I suppose I shouldn't be greedy and expect it all at one time, right?"

"I think you have a right to be happy. You've worked hard for this job. I can't believe that love isn't somewhere in your future too."

"Thanks, Peggy." Hunter squealed out of the parking lot. "Sam put the GPS coordinates into the car for this storage place we're going. What are we looking for? Treasure, I hope, and not a dead body."

"Probably neither one." Peggy grabbed the door handle as Hunter made a sharp turn and revved the Camaro's new engine as she darted in and out of traffic. "I already found the dead body. This is looking for information about what killed him."

"That doesn't sound very exciting." Hunter glanced at her and sailed through a red light. "I really liked the times we've worked together. But I remember them being more on edge, you know?"

Peggy saw the blue and white lights coming up fast behind them. There was a short burst from the police siren.

Hunter glanced into the rearview mirror. "Uh-oh. Don't worry. Once they see that I'm a lawyer, they leave me alone." She pulled the car to the side of the busy road and stopped. "They don't want to irritate someone they might need later."

"Do you need your registration?" Peggy asked.

"It won't matter." Hunter grinned and then put a finger to her mouth for quiet as the officer approached her window.

"License and registration, please."

Peggy recognized him. "Hello, Officer Blandiss—Luke! We met yesterday."

Luke Blandiss leaned into the car a few inches and smiled at her. "Dr. Lee. Good to see you. I hope you aren't being kidnapped."

"Oh no. My friend, Hunter, is taking me to an appointment. How are you this morning?"

"I'm great, thanks."

Hunter handed him her business card from the prestigious law firm where she worked. "This should take care of it, Officer."

He looked at the business card and handed it back to her. "I really need your driver's license, Ms. Ollson, and your registration. Do you know why I stopped you?"

"Because you didn't have anything else to do?" Hunter joked.

Luke looked a little put out. "No, ma'am. You were speeding, driving erratically, and failed to stop for a red light."

"I am an officer of the court, sir. That allows me some leeway in these matters."

"Maybe I should get the registration out now," Peggy suggested.

"That isn't necessary," Hunter said.

"I'm afraid it is, ma'am," Luke added.

"*Fine.*" Hunter huffed angrily as she dug her driver's license out of her bag. "You might be sorry you did this."

He looked at her license, and Peggy handed him the registration that had been in the glove box. "You're only making it worse, ma'am. You were driving recklessly. That could mean trouble for anyone in your path."

Hunter looked like she was ready to pop. "I think we've established *who* might be in trouble." She snatched her license back from him. "Can I go now?"

He smiled at her in a less than threatening manner. "Not yet. I have to check your information. Be right back."

As he left, Hunter made a strangled sound in the back of her throat. "Am I wrong?" she whispered. "Was he checking *me* out?"

Peggy laughed. "He's very nice."

Hunter pulled down the visor mirror to stare at herself. "And really cute. Did he mention if he was single?"

"No. We didn't have that kind of conversation. But you never know."

Luke came back a few minutes later—after Hunter had refreshed her lipstick and pulled at her shirt to show more cleavage. "I'm going to let you go with a warning this time, Ms. Ollson."

Hunter smiled prettily. "Thank you so much. And please, call me Hunter. You never know. We might work together some time. You're a police officer, and I'm a lawyer."

"But you don't work for the DA's office," he said. "Anyway, I'm giving you a warning, instead of a citation, because you have a safe driving record. Let's keep it that way, hmm?"

"I'll be very careful, Officer." Hunter leaned toward him. "Do police officers ever have drinks with lawyers who aren't in the DA's office?"

"I guess that would all depend on the police officer, and the lawyer."

"What about you and me?" Hunter threw herself right into it.

Luke glanced at the street behind him and grinned at her. "Sure. That could happen. I can't make a date with you because I'm on duty, and I did stop you for a violation. But sometimes I hang out with some friends downtown at Dem Bones. You know it?"

"I sure do. I'll see if I can swing by." Hunter winked at him.

"Okay. Drive safely, Hunter. You might not be so lucky next time." He saluted her and walked back to his car.

Hunter squealed as she pulled out into traffic. "Please tell me he's single!"

"Would you like me to call Paul and ask him?"

"No! That would be going too far." Hunter glanced into the rearview mirror. "He is *such* a babe! I hope he's single."

"I hope so too." Peggy hid her smile as she glanced out

the window.

They finally reached the storage facility. Arnie was leaning against his car, waiting for them. He waved when he saw Peggy.

"I was wondering if you were coming," he said. "I thought you might have changed your mind."

"Not at all. Do you have the code to get in?"

"Why don't you just hop in my car, and I can give you a lift back when we're done," he suggested.

Hunter frowned. "I have strict orders not to leave you, Peggy. Sam made me promise to stay until you were done. We'll follow him in."

Peggy relayed the message. Arnie shrugged and got back into his car. They followed him through the open gate, after he'd punched in the code. Peggy showed Hunter where to park. Arnie parked beside them.

They followed the twists and turns between the buildings until they reached Unit 34. Arnie took out a small key on an orange ring. He glanced at Peggy and then opened the door.

"Well!" Peggy stared in surprise at the open, empty space.

Poinsettia
The Christmas flower. Poinsettias were known as Cuetlaxochitl in Mexico. A sap was used to control fevers, and the bracts (modified leaves) were used to make a reddish dye. Poinsettias don't actually flower, as is commonly thought. The bracts turn red and appear to be flowers amidst the green leaves.

Chapter Fifteen

Arnie drove to the office to demand to know what had happened to the contents of the unit. Hunter and Peggy walked into the small storage building.

"What was supposed to be in here?" Hunter kicked aside a few shreds of paper.

"Files and other things. I'm sure Sam told you that Harry Fletcher supposedly had files he kept on his wife's death." Peggy picked up an old bottle cap from the concrete floor. "He said he had files about John's death too."

Hunter grabbed Peggy's hand. "Your first husband, John? Sam didn't tell me that. Why would this man have files about John?"

"It's a long story. It doesn't seem to matter much right now since everything is gone."

Arnie returned riding in a golf cart with the manager. He used his inhaler as he got out after the vehicle had stopped.

"*You!*" The angry manager pointed at Peggy. "She's the one who tried to break in here. She probably took your stuff."

"I didn't take anything," she denied. Not that she wouldn't have, if she'd had the chance. "Did anyone else have a key to this unit?"

"Of course not," the manager denied. "I gave the only key to Mr. Houck here. I don't know what happened."

"Don't you have a key?" Hunter asked him. "You people always keep keys."

"Sure, I have a key." The manager glared at them. "Are you saying you think *I* took the stuff out of here?"

Peggy stopped the angry cascade of words before it could start. "We're not saying anything. We just want to know what happened to everything that was in here."

"Or I want my money back," Arnie said.

"We have video surveillance." The manager tried to pacify him. "Top notch too. We could take a look at it, and maybe you'd recognize the thief. They say thieves travel in packs."

Peggy knew that dig was for her. She ignored it, and they all got on the golf cart to ride back to the office. She, Hunter, and Arnie sat in the waiting room while the manager retrieved the video.

He returned in a few minutes, his face pink with embarrassment. "I'm real sorry, but it looks like that camera wasn't working last night. All I've got is fuzz. We can call the police. Maybe they can get fingerprints or something. I swear this kind of thing doesn't happen often here. Did you get the renter's insurance?"

Arnie didn't get the insurance—not that any amount of money would have brought back the information they were looking for. The manager apologized a few more times and took Peggy, Hunter, and Arnie back to Unit 34.

"So much for that." Hunter adjusted the strap on her handbag. "What do you want to do now, Peggy?"

"There isn't anything to do about Harry's files. Maybe the man who attacked me in the hospital parking lot got them. Maybe there really was something in there that could prove Ann was murdered. I guess we'll never know."

Hunter put her hand on Peggy's shoulder. "There must be some other way to get that information."

Peggy shook her head. "Not the information about John, but we may have another way to get the information about Ann." She fished around in her bag until she found the permission form. "If you'll sign this, Arnie, we can do the work that needs to be done."

He glanced at the paper. "You want to dig up my sister? That's crazy."

"It may be the only way to prove what happened." Peggy watched him look at it again.

"This seems wrong to me." He balled up the paper and gave it back to her. "I don't want anyone touching Ann again. I'm sorry."

Peggy understood how he felt, but she knew Dorothy would simply get a court order to do what needed to be done. "I'm sorry, Arnie. But one way or another, the medical examiner is going to exhume her."

He took a puff from his inhaler, opened the car door, and got inside. "It's a bad world when you can't even protect your sister after she's been laid to rest. I'm sorry I talked to you at all, Peggy. I'm going home."

As the white Cadillac slid by them, Hunter let out a gasp. "Some people don't do well in this heat. Maybe he's one of them."

"I don't know how I'd feel if they wanted to exhume John's body," Peggy said. "It's such a terrible invasion of privacy. John and Ann have already been so violated."

"Still." Hunter opened the doors to her car. "It makes him seem a little suspicious, doesn't it? If I thought Sam had been murdered, and couldn't prove it, I'd let them dig him up. I think you would too."

* * *

Peggy had Hunter take her to police headquarters in downtown Charlotte. She hoped they were done with her ca, and that Al had a few more answers for her.

Hunter made her promise to mention her to Luke if she saw him. Peggy was happy for her. She seemed so excited about meeting him.

It was better going in the front door of the station than the side door where they took prisoners. Peggy spoke with the sergeant at the desk who'd known John and waited while they sent someone to find Al.

A huge poinsettia on the sergeant's desk still had red bracts and huge green leaves. The branches of the plant were so heavy that they drooped into a weeping shape. It was attractive, in an odd way, but Peggy knew the plant couldn't live like that. It needed to be repotted and possibly cut back a little.

"That might be the biggest poinsettia I've ever seen outside a hothouse," she remarked.

"You like it?" he grunted. "It's yours. I didn't even know what the hell it was. Someone stuck it over here at Christmas, and it kept growing."

"Okay." She didn't know what else to say. She didn't want him to put the poor thing into the trash because she'd noticed it.

"Let me get you a sack for that," he offered, getting up from his chair.

Al showed up as the sergeant presented Peggy with the heavy poinsettia. "What's all that about?"

"No one wanted this poor plant, even though it's had phenomenal growth for a tropical, especially in *this* office."

He laughed. "Are you saying this is a bad environment for plants?"

She directed his gaze to a dead fern that was hanging

by the door. "I'd say that."

"Come on back to my office, and let's talk." He held the door for her as she struggled with the heavy canvas bag holding the plant.

Peggy put the bag on the floor near her feet as she sat down in Al's office. Paper, files, and empty food containers were heaped on his desk. She thought he could do with a good clean.

"From what I can tell, this Houck character isn't into much." He handed her Arnie's file. "He's got a few speeding tickets and a misdemeanor for not paying a court fee—but that was a few years ago. He's clean."

"What about Harry? Anything new?"

"There was no sign of an empty, or full, scotch bottle. I don't know what's up with that yet. He's got a file three inches thick for everything from driving without a license, to breaking and entering charges. He served some time when he was younger, but he's been off our radar for a few years. I don't have a clue yet why anyone would want to kill him."

Peggy explained about the puncture wound and poison Dorothy had found in Harry's body. "You'd better find Ann Fletcher's file too. She's going to be exhumed as part of this."

"Really?" He shivered. "I *hate* when they do that. Is she so sure Ann Fletcher was murdered too?"

"I'm probably to blame for that—though I don't like exhuming the body any more than you do. The same poison that killed Harry was in her body when they autopsied her at the hospital. No one took it any further, but it's there. How can we look the other way?"

"I suppose not. I'll pull what I can find on Fletcher's wife." He scribbled her name on a piece of paper. "I don't think it's much since there wasn't an official investigation."

"I should tell you that Harry's papers were stolen too."

"You mean the ones about John?"

"I mean everything he had in the storage unit. Harry had been saving information he could find about his wife's death too."

"You think this Arnie Houck took them?" He sat back in his chair, hands folded across his stomach.

"Why would he? He already had them. We went there this morning, and everything was gone. The manager said the cameras at that side weren't working so we don't have any idea what happened."

"That's a nice coincidence," he muttered. "Your car isn't quite ready to go. You could hang around a while until it is. Feel like taking a look at some pictures to see if you recognize the man who assaulted you yesterday? Maybe this man is already in the system. I don't know about you, but it would make me feel better if we knew who it was."

"Sure. Dorothy is probably working on that court order. I can look at pictures. Maybe we'll get lucky."

Al heaved his large frame out of the chair and got her settled behind his computer. He found the spot where the digitized pictures of criminals were kept. "Go to it. I'll check on your car."

Peggy had to sit on the very edge of Al's big, leather chair to keep it from rocking back. It nearly swallowed her in its buttery, soft folds. She put one hand on the mouse to scroll through the photos. These were not only local criminals, but also national felons.

It was amazing, after a short time, how much all of them looked the same. She blinked her eyes, and pushed to focus, but it was difficult. Page after page flew by with no sign of the man whose face was etched in her memory.

"Any luck?" Al came back with a cup of coffee for her.

"He might be in here, and I might not recognize him."

"I know what you mean. There are a lot of faces in

there. Try to close your eyes for a minute, and visualize him when he was closest to you. Remember, his hair will probably be different. He might be younger. Just keep looking."

Peggy did as he asked. She scanned four more pages while she drank her coffee. She was about to scroll up again, when one of the faces caught her attention.

Is that him?

She squinted hard at the man's face. His hair was different—shorter. His face was thinner too, but the eyes looked the same. Also the mouth. He'd had a scar right at the corner of his mouth when he'd attacked her. It wasn't in this picture, but Peggy believed it could be him.

His name was Ray Quick. He'd been born in Florence, South Carolina, and had been in and out of trouble most of his life.

She looked closer at the image. The more she looked, the more sure she was that it was him. His description included his height and weight. Five foot nine, one hundred and sixty pounds.

Peggy closed her eyes and envisioned him during their scuffle in the parking lot. He was taller than her, but not as tall as Steve or Paul. The height worked, although she thought he might weigh less than what they had listed.

Al came back a few minutes later, and she showed him the photo. He nodded. "Yeah. Kind of a small-time punk who does jobs for other people. We'll look him up and see if he's in Charlotte. Good catch."

She smiled. "I hope I'm not causing some poor man extra grief by picking his face out of the computer. I could be wrong."

"Let's run with this, and we'll see. If we can find him, we'll bring him in for a line-up. That way you'd see him in the flesh, and it would be what he looks like right now."

"Thanks. I guess I should get back to the office. Is my car ready?"

"Yeah. It's ready to go. I had it taken in front." He handed her the keys. "Be careful, Peggy. I don't like not knowing why you were attacked. He had to know you could go right back in and get another copy of the file he took. That means it was a warning. The next time could be worse."

"I know," she admitted, getting to her feet slowly. She was so stiff from the fall yesterday. It felt like every part of her was bruised. "He probably hoped I was too scared to go back and get another copy."

Al smiled. "But he didn't know how stubborn Peggy Lee is, did he? How are you feeling today, by the way?"

She eased herself forward a few steps. "I'm in good shape, as long as I don't move."

"I've had those days." He kissed her cheek. "I'll talk to you later."

Al had a rookie take the poinsettia out to the car for her. She stopped in her tracks when she saw that her car wasn't covered in red paint. Al had gotten it cleaned, and the inside was even spotless because of the crime scene work.

She got in the car, texted her thanks to Al, and put the passenger seatbelt around the plant. She was about to drive toward the ME's office when she got a call from Dorothy. A judge had issued a court order for the exhumation at three p.m. Dorothy couldn't be there and asked Peggy if she would mind taking her place.

"Of course," Peggy said, though she would rather be anywhere than at the cemetery.

"Thanks. I'll send you the name of the cemetery, and where you need to meet them when you get there. Talk to you later."

Peggy started the car and drove to The Potting Shed. She might as well take advantage of her time away from the case to relax with her plants and customers. She could also take a peek at lecture for tomorrow at the university. She'd given the same lecture so many times that she tended to take it for granted. It couldn't hurt to look it over.

"And you, my new friend, can be repotted so you can spend the rest of your life at the shop. People will fall in love with you when they see how magnificent you are." She patted the poinsettia carefully.

Selena was surprised to see Peggy at The Potting Shed that morning. She was sorting through another shipment of bulbs, trying to organize them. "What are you doing here?"

"I work here." Peggy put her bag away and put on her apron. "I thought I was here enough that you'd remember that part."

"Ha-ha. You know what I mean. Usually when you're hot on the trail of some bad guy, we get neglected. I'm used to it."

Peggy hugged her. "Not right now. I have to leave to be at an exhumation at three, but I'm here until then."

Selena frowned. "Exhumation? You mean you're digging someone up?"

"I'm afraid so." Peggy started sorting through the bulbs too. "There seems to be no other way to figure out what happened to this poor woman."

"Wow. I didn't know you did things like that. Can I come too?"

.

Chocolate Vines
These exotic plants grow leathery, green leaves. The pulp is edible and likened in taste to tapioca. The chocolate vine plant is visually stunning with its purple flowers and has a wonderful chocolate scent. Large seedpods ripen in mid to late fall. The vine climbs walls, fences, or anything upright.

Chapter Sixteen

Peggy felt blessed that she didn't have to answer that question. Only Selena would want to go out to a cemetery and dig up a woman who'd been dead for twenty years. She talked with the customer who came in looking for something new for her garden and pretended that she hadn't heard the question.

Mary Ann Polumbo was looking for an unusual vine that she could train to climb a new trellis on her gazebo. "I know there are plenty of tried and true plants I could use," she explained. "I see those new exciting plants in the garden catalogues, and I just want one."

"I understand. I feel the same way. And I might have something for you. Come back here with me." Peggy led her to the back of the shop where new plants were kept. "We just got this in. They call it a chocolate vine. Smell it."

"Wow! It smells just like chocolate," Mary Ann raved. "What are these little pods on it?"

"Edible fruit." Peggy pulled one off for her. "Have a taste."

"Are you sure? I've been to your poison plant seminars. Is this safe?"

Peggy popped one into her own mouth. "Very safe. And very delicious."

Mary Ann pulled off another pod and chewed it. "I love this! How many could I grow on my new gazebo?"

"I would think two or three. You don't want to be overwhelmed by them. Aren't they fantastic?"

"You always have what I'm looking for, Peggy. I'll take three, if you have them. Can I plant them now?"

"Yes. But they may lose the flowers and pods. They'll come back next year."

"Wonderful. Thanks so much. What would I do without you?"

The three chocolate vines were actually for one of Sam's projects. Peggy let Selena ring up Mary Ann's order while she got on the Internet and ordered five more. It looked like chocolate vines might be popular.

Selena carefully wrapped the vines and helped Mary Ann take them out to her car.

Peggy started back sorting bulbs. This was the bad part about getting them wholesale. They came in one large box with stickers showing which was which. If she put them all out together, the customers got confused. It was worth the time and trouble to separate them.

Mr. Beazle came in with his usual sour expression. Peggy and Selena always joked that he reminded them of Ebenezer Scrooge. He always dressed in an old black suit and frequently complained. Usually he was looking for the cheapest sale plants.

Selena ran into the back of the shop before she had to wait on him.

Peggy smiled, as she always did, and went to ask him what she could do.

"There were three of the five tulip bulbs I bought from you last fall that did *not* bloom this spring." He glared at her over his starched white collar. "What do you plan to do about it?"

"I plan to give you three new bulbs," she replied, trying not to lose her patience with him. "Would you like more tulip bulbs?"

"That would be all right—but not red. I have far too many red tulips."

"All right." She grabbed a small brown bag and put three yellow tulip bulbs into it. "Is that all?"

"I might be interested in a new rose bush for my formal garden area."

"This isn't really a good time to plant roses, Mr. Beazle. I can't guarantee they'll grow."

"Inferior products, madam. You should be able to plant them at *any* time with success."

"You've been a gardener for a long time," she reminded him. "The dog days of summer aren't a good time to plant many things."

"Superstitious hogwash!"

"Have it your way." She shrugged. "I'll sell you a rose bush, but I won't guarantee it."

"Why would I purchase it from *you* then?" He grabbed his bag of tulip bulbs and left the store.

Peggy sighed as she sat in her rocker. She was glad all of her customers weren't like him.

Selena glanced around before walking to the counter. "That is one mean, old dude. I wish he'd find another garden shop."

"Thanks for running off and leaving me with him."

"You could just ban him from The Potting Shed, and we wouldn't have that problem."

"We can't always work with people we like."

Selena snorted. "That's the truth. Look at Sam."

"I think you're jealous of him."

"Jealous? Why?"

"Because everyone loves him and asks for him." Peggy got up to pull a dead catkin from the miniature cattail plant that grew in the pond. "It's either that, or you're in love with him."

"Both of those ideas are stupid," Selena argued, but her cheeks bloomed with red. "Sam is gay. He isn't interested in me that way."

Peggy shook her head. "That doesn't mean you aren't interested in him that way."

"Trust me. I can go out with whoever I want, whenever I want. I don't have to sit around sighing over Sam like those other women. They're so pathetic." Selena glanced at her watch. "Speaking of which, I'm going to take a break and get something at the Kozy Kettle. Want something?"

"No, thanks. Have fun."

Did Selena have a crush on Sam? That could lead to all kinds of difficulties. She needed them to be able to work together, but she knew the heart wasn't always predictable. It might be a good idea to talk to Sam. He was a few years older, and in most cases, very mature. She'd have to hope he could take what she had to say seriously, without making fun of Selena.

The door chimed, and Peggy looked up. It was Arnie again. He stepped inside and used his inhaler.

"I suppose you're surprised to see me." He smiled. "I'm surprised to be here."

"Why are you here?"

"It's about the idea of digging up my sister." He took a seat in the chair by the door. "I'm sorry I was so upset about the idea earlier. I wasn't expecting it. I've thought about it. If you think it's important, I'll sign that paper."

Peggy felt bad that he'd come to tell her he'd reconsidered. She'd warned him that they would do it without his permission. Now she was embarrassed to tell him that it was already done.

"I'm sorry, Arnie. The medical examiner already got a court order. They're exhuming Ann's body this afternoon at three. When they think a murder might have been covered up, they move pretty quickly."

"I suppose I should've known." He got up from the chair. "Will you be there?"

"Yes."

"I will be too. Thanks, Peggy."

She watched him walk outside. At least no one had tried to tell her that John's death was an accident. She knew from the beginning that he was murdered. Maybe she'd be smart to let it go at that. What difference did it make *why* he was killed? He was dead—that was all that really mattered. She didn't want to see him exhumed too.

Her cell phone rang. It was Paul. "Hi, Mom. I need to talk to you. Do you have some free time?"

"I'm at The Potting Shed. Could you come here?"

After a short pause, he said, "I can't. Not the house either. We need to meet somewhere that people wouldn't expect you to be."

Peggy's cinnamon-colored brows knit together. "Where are you? What's wrong? Who are you worried about seeing?"

"Steve. Maybe Al. Meet me at the Old Settler's Cemetery. Can you get there by eleven?"

"Yes. But what's going on, Paul? I don't like the way you sound."

"Just meet me there, Mom, please."

Peggy put down her cell phone as the call ended. Something was wrong. She hadn't heard Paul sound that way since he got in trouble at college for helping a friend pass an exam.

She looked at her watch. It was ten-fifteen. She could see Selena coming back to the shop with her hands full of goodies. Since she'd had a chance to take a break, maybe she wouldn't feel so bad about Peggy leaving for a while.

Peggy was telling Selena that she had to leave before eleven, when a man pulling a small wagon with a huge watermelon in it came into the shop.

"Miss Peggy." Dorian Hubbard pulled at his cap. "I thought you might be interested to see my prize-winning watermelon. I bought the seeds right here. Someone from the Observer is on his way to take pictures."

Peggy marveled at the watermelon, rubbing her hands on the smooth round sides. "How much does it weigh?"

"Seventy-eight pounds." Dorian was a long-time customer. "I thought you all could use a little extra publicity."

"Thank you for thinking of us." Peggy was always surprised at the kindness and thoughtfulness of her customers.

"I've got some mighty big squash this year too." He sat down in the chair by the door, took off his hat, and swiped his hand across his sweaty brow. "Hot out there. Those squalls in the Atlantic don't do much good for us up here."

Selena stood close to Peggy. "You can't go anywhere until the reporter comes. I'm not getting my picture taken with Godzilla the watermelon."

"Don't worry," Peggy whispered back. "I'll be late if I have to."

They sat around talking about gardens and the many bumper crops they'd heard about that summer. Dorian said he'd gone to the county farmer's market, and a man had offered him a hundred dollars for his watermelon.

"That got me thinking. If he was interested in it, maybe someone else would be too. I called the Charlotte Observer, and the young man I talked to was right excited by it."

It was ten-thirty, but there was no sign of the reporter.

Selena got Dorian a cup of cold water and started working on the bulbs again. Peggy talked with her guest and kept looking at her watch. She was worried, after talking to Paul. She wished he would've said a little more about what was wrong.

A young man in a blue T-shirt and jeans carrying a large camera finally came into the shop. He saw Dorian and the watermelon. "Hi. I'm Skip Taylor. I guess this is the big fella."

Dorian pulled on his suspenders as he got to his feet. "That's right. Never grew one like it before. Peggy sold me the seeds. This is her garden shop. Make sure you get the name right—The Potting Shed."

Skip wrote the information in his notepad. He shook hands with Peggy. "I'm glad to meet you. Nice place."

"Thank you. But really, Dorian is more responsible for the big watermelon because he's such a good gardener. He takes good care of his garden."

"So, we think the garden is more important than the seed?" Skip asked.

"Not as far as I'm concerned," Dorian denied. "Look around you, young man, do you see any other garden shops in this area?"

Sam came in as Skip was trying to think of any other garden shops at all. Once Sam got the idea that The Potting Shed was getting free publicity—he took over the event—making sure the reporter knew they did landscaping too. He had Skip take pictures of all three of them with the big watermelon—setting it up so that the photo would pick up the contents of the shop behind them.

"He's much better at this than I ever was," Peggy confided to Dorian as Sam had Skip taking pictures all over the shop while he gave him information.

"But you're a damn sight better looking." Dorian winked at her. "You know, a few years back, I thought there might be something between you and me. We both love plants, and we lost our spouses. Then that good-looking fella came along and snatched you up. I should've done it quicker."

Peggy hugged him. He'd been one of her first customers and had always been there to support her. "I didn't know you felt that way. I'm flattered. We could've grown some big vegetables together."

Dorian's laugh was wheezy, reminding her of Arnie. She glanced at her watch. It was five minutes until eleven. Sam had this. She was going to meet Paul.

She said goodbye to Dorian and thanked him again for bringing the newspaper to her door. Selena waved to her as she was leaving.

Sofia was standing with her nose pushed against the plate glass at the front of the shop. "Is that a newspaper reporter? Emil saw him go in with a camera."

"Yes. Maybe you should see if he'd be interested in taking pictures of your shop too."

"You're right! I better go tell Emil."

Peggy watched her run back across the courtyard. Skip Taylor might be in for a full day of taking pictures and reporting on the shops in Brevard Court. She got in her car and raced through downtown Charlotte, hoping none of the blue and white squad cars would notice.

She was only a few minutes from the old Settler's Cemetery on Fifth Street. It was maintained by the city as a park where workers from downtown could wander and eat lunch each day. The big oak trees overhung the neat paths creating quiet spaces to get away from the bustle of the city.

The cemetery was first used in 1776. Many of the area's Revolutionary War heroes were buried here. The old tombstones told their tales of Charlotte's early settlers who'd brought so much to the fledgling community.

Peggy parked her car on the street and went to search for Paul. She was a few minutes late. She hoped he'd waited for her. When she finally saw him, she waved and walked quickly to meet him.

"Mom." His face was grim. "I've done something you're not going to be happy about. I'm not happy about it either. It just happened."

"What? What just happened?"

Their green gazes locked as he confessed. "I took everything out of Harry Fletcher's storage shed."

Gladiolus
Cultivated since the 1800s, Victorian gardeners, including Monet and Gertrude Jekyll, adored these flowers with their tall, spiky heads, and glorious colors. They bloom best in full sun and will multiply abundantly.

Chapter Seventeen

"What were you thinking, Paul? Why did you steal everything in there?" Peggy couldn't believe her son had done something like this.

"I don't know. You told me about the files you thought might have something to do with Dad. I was thinking about it. Then I came up with a plan."

Paul wasn't in uniform. He wore a plain UNCC T-shirt and jeans. He didn't look like he'd slept well. His eyes were troubled.

"You'll have to put it all back," she decided. "The surveillance cameras weren't working. They don't have a picture of you."

He shrugged. "I wasn't going to let them make a video with me as the star."

"Okay. I guess you can fix the cameras too, when you take Arnie's stuff back to the storage unit."

"Don't you even want to know what was in it?" he asked impatiently.

"Of course I want to know. I assume you went through

Harry's files."

"There were two boxes of files. Most of them were dedicated to information he'd collected about his wife. There were only two folders that had information about Dad."

Peggy sat on one of the benches. "What did you find?"

Paul sat beside her. "Not much. Harry found out that Dad was helping Steve and another FBI agent look into a series of murders in Charlotte. It looked like they believed a state senator's death was related. It didn't make much sense."

"What senator? Was he murdered?"

"No, but he *did* die in a car wreck at around the same time. His name was Senator Richard Malcolm. I looked it up. There was no mention of Dad or any kind of conspiracy."

Peggy took a deep breath, trying to dispel the pain that ached in her chest. "I don't see what the link would be between them."

"Me either—not yet anyway. But Mom, this private detective knew all about this while we were kept in the dark all this time. That's not right. I think we should talk to Steve and Al about it. There might be more that they're not telling us."

"I don't think that's true," she disagreed. "I'm sure they've told us all they could."

Paul wasn't convinced. "I want to ask them."

"All right." Peggy watched three pretty young girls in flowered, summer dresses walk by them. "Do you need help taking the stuff back to the storage shed?"

"No. I've got this. Do you want me to make copies of the information about Harry's wife?"

"You don't have to. I'm sure Arnie will share it with me—if he can find it."

"I'm sorry about this. I wasn't thinking straight."

She smiled and patted his hand. "I thought you were a little too calm when we talked about it. I should've known something was up."

"Yeah. Dad's death is one thing I can't be calm about. All these years—I believed something was up with him dying that way. Al kept telling me it was okay. I never believed him. I was right. I guess he lied to me."

"I don't think Al knew anything about this other stuff with the FBI. He told me he didn't even know John was working with them. I believe him."

"I don't know what I believe now." His eyes focused on hers. "What about Steve? I feel kind of weird knowing he was working with Dad when he was killed, and then suddenly he marries you. Don't you think that's kind of strange?"

Steve had told Peggy after they were married that he'd been keeping an eye on her after John was killed. The FBI was worried that she might be a target too. He'd told her that he'd fallen in love with her—despite the almost ten-year age gap between them.

She believed him, and she trusted him. She knew it was hard to convey trust between two people to a third party like Paul. "The whole thing sounds odd, but I think it makes sense. I know Steve. And it wasn't as if the day after your father died he came knocking at my door looking for a date. Let's give him some credit."

Paul ran his hand through his spikey red hair. "I know you're right. Steve is a good guy. I know he wasn't involved in Dad's death, except as his contact with the Bureau. Al told me he's worked with the FBI before too. It happens in local cases."

He got to his feet. "I made copies of all the papers Harry had about Dad. I didn't want to take a chance on losing them, even though they don't really make any difference as far as I can tell. I just want them, you know?"

She got up and hugged him. "I know. I'm sure I'll get the originals after you put everything else back in the storage unit."

"Yeah. I'll take care of that tonight. I don't know how you'll play this with Arnie. You'll have to convince him to look at it again without giving anything away."

"Don't worry. I'll think of something. In the meantime, please give up your cat burglar tendencies."

"I've sworn off. Mai would kill me if she found out."

They were about to go their separate ways when Peggy thought to ask about what else was in the storage shed.

"More files. I didn't read all of them. Some personal things like clothes and books. They looked like they belonged to Harry's wife. You know, there were some books on plants and poisons that you'd probably like. She must've been a gardener too."

"Really?" Peggy thought about Ann's unusual death. "If I have a chance, I'll look at them. Thanks, Paul. Be careful."

Peggy went back to her car, thinking about the idea that Ann could have been responsible for her own death. People read about herbs and plants that could be used for medicine without realizing that the tinctures and formulas had to be followed as closely for home remedies as with drugs.

Maybe it was possible Ann had accidentally killed herself. The first thing every poison expert learned is that what can kill can usually heal, and vice versa. Had Ann been treating herself for some health problem and overdone it?

Whatever answer that might bring wouldn't work with what had happened to Harry. Ann had been dead for a long time. In Peggy's experience, people didn't come back from the dead to kill others.

On the other hand, Arnie might share his sister's curiosity about poisons and plants. Even though his record was clear, it was always possible that he could have finally decided to take revenge for his sister.

If Paul could do something so irresponsible for information about John's death, it was certainly possible that Arnie could have taken it one step further.

Peggy thoughtfully drove back to The Potting Shed. She spent as much time as she could there helping Selena with the new bulbs and talking with customers. She wasn't looking forward to heading to the cemetery for the exhumation. She was sure that was what made the time fly by.

Before she left, she spoke with Sam about Selena.

He scoffed when she told him the girl might have feelings for him. "That's crazy. She's like my little annoying sister. We've known each other a long time, Peggy. She knows how I feel."

"Believe it or not, women don't care if men are gay. They believe they'll change for them. I just have a feeling there's something more going on with Selena right now. Maybe you could say something to her."

Sam arched a blond brow in his tanned face. "Something like what?"

"Pretend she's Hunter. Say something to her that you might say to your younger sister."

"You're really messing with my head today." He grinned. "First you tell me Selena might feel romantic toward me, and then you tell me to talk to her like she was Hunter. That's just *so* wrong."

"You know what I mean. I know you'll figure it out." She waved to him as she left the shop. "I don't want to be late for my first exhumation."

"Yeah. I don't blame you," he yelled back.

Peggy saw Arnie's white Cadillac parked next to the maintenance crew's vehicle before she pulled into the cemetery. A Charlotte/Mecklenburg police cruiser followed her in and parked behind her. Two men, dressed in blue coveralls, held shovels as they stood beside a yellow backhoe next to a grave.

Everyone was looking at her as she got out of her car, and started across the green grass. She wished she'd told Dorothy that she couldn't be there. It was an uncomfortable feeling.

"You don't have to be here," she said to Arnie. "I don't want to be here, and she wasn't my sister."

"Would you want them to dig up your husband without being there?" he countered.

"Actually, yes. I think I would. Some things are just too painful." She hoped that never happened.

"You from the medical examiner's office?" the police officer asked. "I have the court order. I guess we can get going."

"Yes," Peggy said. "Let's get this over with."

Pine
Pine trees have been around for millions of years. It has been found that the loblolly pine has a long genome that is more than seven times the size of the human genome. There are more than a hundred different species of pine.

Chapter Eighteen

It took about an hour to dig up Ann Fletcher's coffin. Peggy rode back to the morgue with the dirty coffin in the medical examiner's van. Arnie agreed to make the round trip back with his car so that Peggy could come back for hers. She had promised him information as they got it from the autopsy Dorothy would do on his sister.

Peggy sat on the narrow bench, staring at the faded, gray coffin. She hoped something good would come of this for Arnie and his sister. It also made her wish she'd had John cremated.

Dorothy was waiting at the back of the office where the bodies were taken in from the loading ramp. The two men who'd come from the morgue got the heavy coffin on a gurney and rolled it inside.

"How did it go?" Dorothy searched Peggy's face.

"Everything went as well as it could," Peggy responded. "Dorothy, this is Ann Fletcher's brother, Arnie. He was out there with us. Arnie, this is the medical examiner, Dorothy Beck."

Dorothy shook Arnie's hand. "I'm so sorry it had to come to this. I know it's never easy."

"If it helps find the truth about what happened to my sister, it will be worth it."

"He's going to take me back to get my car," Peggy explained. "I didn't realize I'd have to ride back with the coffin."

"Sure. You can't beat protocol. I'm going to get started on the autopsy. Maybe I'll have something when you get back." Dorothy nodded and said goodbye to Arnie before she walked back inside the building.

"So you know for sure that Harry was killed by this poison." Arnie held the door to the Cadillac open for Peggy.

"Yes. According to the original autopsy, there was convallatoxin in your sister's body too. Not as much as in Harry's, but we think the delivery method may have been different."

"My sister was really into plants and herbs." Arnie started the car. "She wanted to be an herbalist, or something like that. She had dozens of books on the subject."

Peggy hoped those books were on their way back to Arnie's storage shed. Paul might have to wait until dark to put everything back. Even though what he'd done had been stupid, she understood, and hoped he wasn't caught setting it right.

"It's possible she used lily of the valley on herself," Peggy said. "Do you know if she had anything wrong with her?"

He shrugged as he kept his eyes on traffic. "Not really. We weren't as close after she married Harry. It seems to me she might've used it as a sedative, if that's possible. They had a rough life together."

"It isn't used frequently, but it could be something someone might play around with. It's deadly, especially in large doses, or prolonged use."

"But Ann has been dead for a long time. Do you think Harry poisoned her twenty years ago and then poisoned himself?"

"Not really. I think this may have been done by a third person." She stared at the side of his face as he maneuvered the big car through the city.

He glanced at her. "You're not thinking I did it, are you? I don't know anything about that stuff. I sure don't know why you wouldn't just shoot a person rather than go through all that trouble. And I *didn't* kill my own sister."

"I frequently wonder why anyone uses poison too. It's a lot more common than most people realize." Peggy looked away from him. Now might not be the best time to get the truth out of him. If he had killed Harry, she'd be better off proving that with her knowledge and letting the police take over.

They reached the cemetery, and Peggy got in her car. Arnie reminded her that she'd promised updates on his sister. He pulled off, with an abrupt wave, before she was ready to go.

Probably a little put out that I sounded as though he might have killed Ann.

This was the same cemetery where John was buried, the largest in the city. She hadn't visited his grave in a long time. Right after he'd been killed—and for the first year—she and Paul had come out here every Sunday. After a while, it just felt wrong. She was more comfortable thinking about him at home in the garden than lying here with a stone at his head.

Today, she decided to make an exception.

It was funny how some things were never forgotten. Even though it had been years since she'd been to John's grave, she was able to walk right to it without a second thought. She remembered the old knotty pine that grew close to it. The tree was still there, squat and twisted, but beautiful. It was probably at least 100 years old.

John's headstone had accumulated some moss but otherwise looked the same. The cemetery put plastic plants on the grave a few times a year. The plastic ivy in the red clay pot looked cheap. Maybe she'd ask them not to do that anymore. The grass was all cut to the same height on the grave and around it. She sat down on a nearby cement bench and stared at the spot.

"This is silly," she said. "I know you aren't in there. I'm sure if you're anywhere, you're at home with that big, lopsided azalea you planted. That's why I stopped coming. I didn't want Paul to remember you being dead. I didn't want to either. I like to think that you're working in some celestial garden. I'd rather think of you that way, John. I hope that's okay."

A warm breeze rustled through the old oaks and pines. Somewhere beyond her line of vision, a dog was barking. Cars whizzed by the cemetery on the main road, and a plane roared through the blue sky above her.

"I'm going now, John. I love you. Even though talking to you here is stupid, I can't seem to help myself. I'll see you at home." She kissed her fingers and laid them on the top of his headstone.

There were a few other people walking through the large cemetery, but mostly it was empty. The majority of people probably visited on the weekend. Peggy walked quickly around the other graves, taking note of the large hole still open where they'd dug up Ann's coffin. It was surrounded by yellow police tape and signs warning everyone to stay away.

As she approached the car, her cell phone rang. It was Dorothy.

"Peggy, you should get back here right away. There's something you have to see."

"I'm on my way." She put her phone in her bag and got in the car.

* * *

Peggy parked in the morgue parking lot, reminding herself that she'd have to put her bike in the back of the car to take it home that day.

Dorothy was waiting in her office, going through some information on her computer. "I thought you'd never get back."

"I wasn't gone that long. How much information could you get from the body in that amount of time?"

"Come with me. You'll be surprised."

This was Peggy's first exhumed body autopsy. She wasn't looking forward to it. It was bad enough looking at a dead body that had recently died. She didn't want to think about what it would be like to examine someone who'd been dead twenty years.

Both women put on masks and gloves before they entered the autopsy room. Dorothy was like a small child with a surprise, almost skipping away from her office and down the long hall.

"I planned to look for the mark on the back of the neck indicating that Mrs. Fletcher had been injected with poison," Dorothy explained.

Peggy stared at the body, trying to look away from the desiccated form on the table. There was already the large 'Y' incision across the chest. No fresh marks had been made. Dorothy had only started.

"I found a mark. It's difficult to say if it is an injection site, but a cursory examination using Mrs. Fletcher's records told me something very important."

"What?" Peggy shook her gaze away from the body.

"This *isn't* Ann Fletcher." Dorothy's voice was excited.

Even though Peggy couldn't see her grin from behind the facemask, she knew Dorothy well enough to know it was there.

"What are you talking about?"

"I had to check it twice," Dorothy continued. "Some people don't have anything that can separate them from other people, especially in this state of decomp. Although, she *is* very well preserved."

"So you checked it twice, and what did you find?"

"No surgical change of the chest area. Ann Fletcher was born with a deformity that made her ribcage curve into her heart. She had surgery to repair that when she was twelve years old. When you look at the x-ray for this body, it never occurred. Unless her medical records are wrong, this has to be another woman."

Peggy couldn't believe it. "Are you sure?"

"Look at the x-rays." Dorothy pointed to the pictures on the lighted board. "I don't have a copy of Ann's chest x-rays yet, but I've already called the hospital in Columbia for it."

"Do you want me to call Arnie and ask him to verify that they were living there at the time?"

"No. Let's see what they have. Her driver's license and birth certificate are from there. I think we'll find her hospital records there too. Better not to involve a possible suspect."

"You think Arnie is a suspect?"

Dorothy put her hand on Peggy's arm. "Don't feel bad. We can't know for sure until it all comes out in the wash."

Peggy didn't feel bad. Arnie was a likely suspect since he had ties to both people. "How are you going to determine who this woman is, if she isn't Ann Fletcher?"

"I was able to get some prints from her. I'm hoping she's in the system—for whatever reason. If not, we'll have to rely on the usual channels of searching for women of her description who disappeared at about the same time Mrs. Fletcher was thought to have died."

"What about the convallatoxin?"

"Well, there's no blood, so we'll have to do tissue samples. I'll let you know what we find."

"All right. This wasn't the news I was expecting, Dorothy, but thanks for telling me." Peggy glanced at her watch. "I was going to have my assistant at the garden shop take care of our garden club meeting, but since I'm at a loose end here, I might as well take care of it myself."

"I'll get back with you as soon as we have any further updates. Take care."

"I will. Thanks." Peggy took off her white coat and hung it up near her desk before she left.

It wasn't easy getting her bike into the car. She finally had to skip the trunk and push it into the backseat. The hybrid got great gas mileage—some days she didn't even have to switch over from electric. But it wasn't meant to hold more than a few bags of groceries.

There was plenty of time to take the car home and ride her bike to the shop. Even though traffic could be tricky, she liked riding when the weather was nice. She didn't expect to go anywhere else but the shop and home again. Riding to the ME's office, and the shop, and then home could be exhausting.

The roofers were working on the house when she got back. It was driving Shakespeare crazy to have them up there. She could hear him from outside as he ran back and forth through the house, barking loudly.

"Peggy." Dalton Lee was standing in the drive when she got out of the car. "I hope that animal of yours doesn't cause any damage inside the house."

"Dalton. I haven't seen you for a while. How is the vinegar working on getting rid of the ivy on the roof?"

"Not as good as a chemical would have, but I

understand your concerns about the other foliage. The magnificent work you and John did here should be preserved. For once, we are in agreement."

Peggy had found through the years that, if she squinted hard enough, she could see a little of John in his uncle's face. They were about the same height and build. Dalton's hair had gone white though the years, and there were more wrinkles. But seeing her husband in him made dealing with him a little easier.

"I heard you retired from your law firm last month."

"Semi-retired." Dalton narrowed his blue eyes as he put one hand across his brow to shade his gaze from the sun. "I'm not the kind to play golf twenty-four hours a day."

"That doesn't surprise me."

"I heard something disturbing about John, Peggy." His gaze shifted from the work being done on the roof to her face. "What's this about you hiring a private detective to look into John's death?"

Peggy smiled. "That's what happens when you don't get the information from the source. I *didn't* hire a private detective. I was working on another case with one who claimed to have some knowledge of why John was killed."

The disbelieving expression on Dalton's face was comical. "If you have money you want to throw away, you should donate it to a charity. We all know why John was killed. What more knowledge do you need about it?"

"John was working with the FBI at the time of his death. Did you know that? Some people think his death wasn't the random act of violence that it seemed."

"The FBI? Who told you that, Peggy? I suppose that was your private detective."

"No. It was the FBI. John's case is still open with them, and with the police. They're still trying to find out why John was killed. They think John had information that his killers didn't want to get back to John's FBI partner." She didn't plan to mention that John's partner had been Steve.

Dalton shook his head. "Why would John have done something like that? Wasn't it foolhardy enough that he was a police detective? I can't think what possessed him to take up that career."

"You were very clear about that when John was alive. You obviously didn't know him very well. He wanted to help people. This was his way."

"I've helped people my whole life as a lawyer. No one has ever shot at me. John was reckless, or he'd still be alive today."

Peggy started to explain further.

He cut her off. "Never mind. I don't want to know anything else about it. I'm going to talk to the foreman of the roofing company. I'll see you later."

"Bye." Peggy shook her head. Same old Dalton. At least he hadn't reminded her, as he usually did, that John's cousin would be back someday to take the house from her. Not that it was true—John's cousin wasn't interested in the house yet. She knew Dalton just liked to rub it in that the house and property weren't hers.

With a sigh, Peggy took her bike out of the car. She went inside for her riding satchel that she used to carry her handbag, and other necessary supplies, over her shoulder.

Shakespeare was whining as he heard the roofers walking across the ceiling. She tried to comfort him, but the noise was threatening. Peggy put him in the basement with her plants so that the sound would be baffled. He curled up on a rubber mat and closed his eyes.

"Don't make me regret this," she said as she stroked his head. "No bouncing around, upsetting the plants. Okay?"

His doggy snore was her only answer.

Oh well. She went back upstairs. She could only hope Shakespeare and her plants would cohabitate peacefully while she was gone. She put on new lipstick, grabbed a power bar in case she missed dinner, set the alarm, and went out to her bike.

Most people were headed home at this time of day, but traffic was bad going both ways. Peggy kept her bike close to the edge of the road. There seemed to be some drivers who just didn't want to share the road. They veered too close to her and even honked their horns and yelled obscenities.

As much work as Charlotte had put into making bike riding friendly with cars on city streets, it was still not quite acceptable.

Peggy reached Brevard Court as Selena was closing down for the day. They held the garden club at the Kozy Kettle so that members could enjoy snacks and drinks—and it was good for Emil and Sofia too.

"I thought you weren't going to be here." Selena picked up the tray of flowers that Peggy had made up for the club. "Did you already dig up the body?"

"Yes. They didn't need me afterward, so I thought I might as well come back here and take care of the garden club so you can go home."

Selena tapped her chin as though she was considering a complex physics problem. "But what will I do with myself? Working for you is my *life*."

Peggy took the tray from her. "Then you definitely need some time off."

"I was sure of that today when Sam started giving me a lecture on men I should be trying to date. Any idea what caused that?"

"Afraid not. I have to go. Thanks for everything. Have a good night."

Peggy shook her head as she walked across the courtyard to the Kozy Kettle. *Sam!*

Emil opened the door for her. The wonderful smell of baking croissants, shortbread, and chocolate chip cookies almost picked her up off the floor. Her stomach growled, and she knew she was going to have to eat something besides the power bar in her bag.

"Come in, come in!" Sofia was moving through the small crowd of gardeners with samples to make them hungry. "Would you like some tea? Emil, make Peggy some tea."

"I will." Emil moved close to Peggy. "How was it—digging up the body?"

"It was as bad as you'd expect. We can only hope to solve the mystery of what killed the poor woman." Peggy didn't even bother asking how he knew.

"I helped dig up one of my cousins when I was a teenager." Emil shook his head. "Bad business. His father thought he was a vampire. He was ready to cut off his head and fill his body with garlic."

"Okay. I'll bite." Peggy smiled as she knew she was in for one of his fantastic stories. "What happened?"

"My cousin was too smart for us. He changed into a bat as we opened his coffin. He flew around and around until he disappeared. No one ever saw him again."

"That's amazing," Peggy said. "Looks like we have a good crowd for garden club tonight."

"You know it." He rubbed his hands together. "That's why we love having you and your friends here with us. Has Sofia thanked you for that privilege yet?"

"More than once. Don't worry. You do so many nice things for me too. That's what friends are for, right?"

He wrapped one meaty arm around her and squeezed hard. "That's right. Sofia and I—we love you. But you should get rid of your husband and meet someone new. That man just isn't right. You need a man who knows his way around a farm. We could all benefit from that."

Emil and Sofia had never thought Steve was good enough for her. Even though she and Steve were married, they were constantly looking for another man for her. She guessed they must know a friendly, single farmer now who they wanted her to date.

Peggy put her tray of flowers down on one of the tables. Her plans were to discuss the language of flowers today. It was a popular subject with her garden club members, and they frequently asked her to repeat it.

The garden club members spoke about exciting happenings with their plants and other gardening projects. Claire Drummond had plenty to say about Sam and encouraged everyone to take advantage of his landscaping services.

Peggy was glad Sam wasn't there. The way Claire made it sound, Sam was doing more than fertilizing her yard and planting new bushes. She knew that wasn't true, but not everyone else did. He would've laughed it off, but she knew he would've been uncomfortable.

"Does anyone have any other projects or news they'd like to share with us before we begin the program?" Peggy asked with a smile, looking up at her lively audience.

Her eyes made contact with one of the few men present. Ray Quick stared back at her with a grin on his tan face.

Tansy
A hardy perennial with a strong odor, tansy has strong antiseptic properties. It was once used to preserve the dead. It is still believed to stop decay. Its name is from the Greek athanatos, which means immortality. Tansy makes good insect repellent. Dried flowers and leaves will keep flies and ants out of your house.

Chapter Nineteen

With so many people around, Peggy wasn't worried about her attacker deciding to sit in on her garden club meeting. It made her nervous, mostly because it meant he was following her activities with a careful eye. She needed to call Al and let him know what was going on. Maybe he could send someone to pick up her antagonist. This could be the identification he was looking for.

Putting it aside for now, she started her program. There would be time later to sneak away and call for help.

"Since the early 1800s, the language of flowers has had a meaning all its own. When it first began, the meanings were silent messages—mostly for lovers—but also to warn away those who were unwanted." Peggy fixed her eyes on Ray Quick as she said it.

He nodded and grinned at her. No remorse.

"At that time, words might not be spoken when meeting a lover to let him or her know how you felt. A lady at a party might let her favorite gentleman know that she cared for him by wearing a white clover in a floral arrangement or tucked into her hair. The clover meant, think of me."

A few women in the audience sighed and giggled at such a romantic gesture.

"A gentleman who wanted to profess his feelings for a lady without words might send her a bouquet that included white jasmine, morning glory, and a red rose. Thus, his lady would know how he felt. She, in turn, could use one of the flowers he'd sent her in her hair or as part of a bouquet that she carried to a party."

"What if a gentleman sent something romantic to a lady, and she didn't return his feelings?" Sharon Crosby asked. She was going through a divorce, and everyone knew it.

"In that case, a lady might carry some tansy with her," Peggy replied. "That would mean the lady was having hostile thoughts toward the man."

Sharon's friend, Diedre, laughed and nudged her with her elbow. "You need to plant a bunch of that around your house, Sharon. Then maybe Tripp might get the idea."

There was some good-natured laughter, but everyone there was on Sharon's side of the divorce. They meant well by it.

"My daughter is planning her wedding," Kim Rogers said with a smile. "She's looking for some unusual plants for her bouquet and the table settings. Any suggestions according to meanings?"

Peggy nodded. "A good wedding bouquet flower, to get away from the usual roses and mums, might be ivy for fidelity, pansy for loving thoughts, and red tulips for a declaration of love. Holly might be good on the tables since it signifies domestic happiness."

Kim wrote down what Peggy said. "Thanks. I'll tell her."

There were dozens of questions about various plants and flowers. Peggy answered them with one eye on Ray Quick, who was drinking a cup of coffee and munching on some chocolate chip cookies.

Part of her wished he'd just go away, while the other part knew he should be in jail after assaulting her. She wanted to see him in jail, although that might only cause someone else to come after her. She already knew he wasn't working alone.

The garden club program was winding down. Peggy's friends were thanking her for doing a program about the language of flowers again. Some were getting ready to go home. Emil and Sofia were beginning to clean up.

Peggy excused herself and ducked behind the tall glass cabinet that held all of the baked goodies each day. She called Al's cell phone, but there was no answer.

Of course.

She knew she could call 911, but it would be difficult to explain what her situation was. Al would know what she was talking about. She thought about calling Steve but hated to drag him into this, as eager as he might be to help her with this problem. There could be complications for him too. An FBI agent probably wasn't supposed to arrest someone for a common assault.

The Kozy Kettle was emptying out quickly as dusk fell across the courtyard outside. Peggy knew she had to do something—Ray Quick was the only one who didn't seem to be in any hurry to leave.

The front door to the shop opened with a light tinkling of a strand of silver bells that Emil had placed over it. Peggy looked through the glass cabinet, hoping it was Ray Quick leaving. Instead, it was Paul.

In one quick whoosh of breath, her heartbeat slowed down, and then revved back up again. What if Ray Quick was carrying a gun and shot Paul? What if her son was killed trying to help her?

Paul saw her looking through the glass and frowned. By then, Ray Quick was the only one there besides his mother, Emil and Sofia. He quickly summed up the situation and moved toward the table where Ray was sitting.

Peggy almost ran out and told her son to leave right away. The words were on her lips as she came around the corner of the glass pastry cabinet.

"Something wrong here?" Paul stood immediately behind Ray. He wasn't wearing his uniform.

"Hey, Paul!" Emil greeted him. "We got coffee and cookies left. Are you feeling hungry?"

In that moment, as Emil and Peggy came out from behind the counter, Ray looked back at Paul. He put his hand into his pocket. Paul moved quickly, pushing the other man forward so that his face was against the table.

"What's happening here?" Emil asked. "Is this man a criminal?"

Paul nodded at Peggy. "Mom? Is this the guy? Or are you sneaking around behind the pastry shelves for the fun of it?"

She put her hand to her chest. She was having a difficult time breathing. "That's him. Be careful. He could be armed."

"What?" Ray held his hand up on either side. "I didn't do anything. I sat in on a flower program. That's not against the law, is it?"

"Not unless you're stalking the woman you assaulted in the hospital parking lot," Paul said as he held on to him. "What's your name?"

"Ray Quick. I think you must have the wrong man, kid."

Paul got him to his feet. "We'll see. Let's go. Call 911, Mom. Anyone got any rope?"

Peggy and Emil walked outside with Paul. Emil carried his baseball bat in case Paul needed his help. Paul put Ray into the backseat of his car, using his belt to secure his hands.

"I guess we showed you, woman hater!" Emil shook the bat at Ray.

"Thanks for your help." Paul shook Emil's hand. "I think we've got this."

"I was glad to help." Emil put his big hand on Peggy's shoulder. "Are you okay? This won't stop you from giving your garden talks at my shop, will it?"

"No. Of course not. If he was looking for me, he would've found me at The Potting Shed too."

"Good! That's good. I'm going back to help Sofia now. See you tomorrow."

Paul and Peggy waited for the police car to arrive.

"How did you know?" she asked him.

He shrugged. "You looked scared. I knew the general description of what the man who attacked you looked like. It was a reasonable guess."

"I'm glad you were there. I was calling for help, but Al was unavailable, and I didn't know how to explain the situation to a 911 operator."

"You could've called Steve," he reminded her.

"I didn't want to get him involved. He has enough on his plate with this big burglary ring he's been chasing. Besides, he might get in trouble coming out for a local issue."

Paul looked skeptical. "Come on, Mom. You know he would've dropped everything to get over here. What's the real story?"

She knew he was right. "He can be a little overprotective. I was afraid he might get paranoid about me coming to the shop."

"That's even crazier." Paul leaned against the car. "I came by to tell you that everything is back at the storage place. I have no idea how you can get your friend to check it out again without giving it away."

"Don't worry." She smiled at him. "I'll think of something. Don't ever do anything like that again. Leave that kind of stuff to private investigators. Police officers don't do that kind of thing."

"Maybe I should become a PI. They get to do all the fun stuff."

Sirens and flashing blue lights heralded a police car sent to pick up Ray. Paul told the officers what had happened and handed him over to them. The officers left with Ray, and Paul walked Peggy back to her bike as he put his belt back on.

"Are you sure you don't want me to put the bike in the car and take you home?" he asked.

"It's not like Ray did anything to me. I'm sure he was just trying to scare me again." She pulled the shoulder strap for her bag across her chest. "I'm going straight home. It shouldn't take more than a few minutes."

"Okay. It suddenly occurs to me how stubborn you are, Mom." He grinned.

"That must be where you get it from." She kissed his cheek and climbed on the bike. "It probably comes as a package deal with the temper and red hair. Love you, sweetie. I'll talk to you later. Say hello to Mai for me."

Peggy rode out into the moderate traffic toward Queens Road. The warm weather was wonderful as the breeze blew through her hair. The ride was mostly uneventful, except for a man in a yellow sports car who cut her off.

She turned into her driveway at home, and a car slowly passed her. Paul smiled and waved. She hadn't realized that he'd followed her home. She knew she should probably be happy that he cared enough to want to make sure she was safe.

Of course, Paul had also called Steve. He was waiting in the yard with Shakespeare after she'd put away her bike. "Nice night," he said.

Shakespeare was subdued in his eagerness to see Peggy. She patted his head and smiled. "Very nice. It was a good ride back from Brevard Court."

"And a good garden club meeting?"

"Stop pretending you don't already know. Paul followed me home. I'm sure he told you all about it." She removed her bag from her shoulder.

"Sounds like you have a stalker."

"Probably not anymore. I plan to press charges against him in the morning. I don't care that he was at the garden club, but he can't go around assaulting people in parking lots."

"I hope Al can get something out of him about this whole situation with Harry Fletcher and his wife. I was thinking about it today while we were on a stakeout for the burglary ring. These people seem really interested in a twenty-year-old death that hasn't even been ruled a murder."

She held the kitchen door open for him. "I know. I think it's fairly conclusive that poison was involved in the death of the woman whose body was autopsied by the hospital. But that body isn't Ann Fletcher. Dorothy found that out today after the body was exhumed."

"Who is it?" Steve took the leash off Shakespeare, and closed the kitchen door.

"We don't know yet. Maybe tomorrow." Peggy sniffed the fragrant air in the kitchen. "You made food. Great. I'm starving."

"I'm glad I'm good for something," he remarked. "Since I'm not good at coming to your rescue because you won't call me when you need help."

"Most women don't call their husbands in that kind of

situation," she apprised him. "They call the police."

"If I quit the FBI and become a police officer—you'll call?" Steve took out two bowls and filled them with the aromatic rosemary vegetable stew he'd made.

Peggy poured them each a glass of iced tea. She put lemon in Steve's glass since he preferred it that way—he was raised in the North. "Don't even joke about it. At least you're more administrative in your job. I don't want to think that you're out there facing people with guns and bad attitudes everyday."

"Okay. I don't want to think about you in that position either. That man tonight could've had a gun. We could be talking about this in the hospital right now."

"All right. I'm sorry. Next time I'm scared, I'll call you. Okay?" She raggedly cut two slices of bakery bread. "Does that work?"

She put the bread on the table beside their bowls, and Steve took her in his arms. "I love you Peggy. I don't want anything to happen to you. Let me help when I can."

Peggy kissed him. "I will. I promise."

Red Maple
The most common tree in North America. Red maple is polygamo-dioecious, which means some trees bear only male or female flowers. On trees with both male and female flowers, the two are on separate branches. Flowers appear in March through May.

Chapter Twenty

The next morning, Peggy got up, showered, and put on a dark suit. It wasn't one of her favorites. She'd come to think of it as her professional costume. She only wore it when she planned to do a lecture at the university. It gave a certain serious element to her dark subject matter.

The suit fit her well, but she'd worn black for so long after John's death. She preferred lighter colors now, especially during the hot summer months.

Steve was up and dressing at the same time. He looked so handsome, freshly shaved, his damp brown hair brushed back from his face. She leaned close and kissed him, feeling his arms tighten around her.

"What was that for?" he asked as he stopped tying his blue tie.

"Because I love you. Where are you off to this morning?"

"My team and I are going to a lecture by a brilliant forensic botanist at a local university." He grinned at her in the mirror. "I hear she's not only well-versed in the subject of poison plants, she's kind of sexy too."

"You'd better be talking about *my* lecture." She smacked his butt.

"Who else?"

"I didn't know you'd be there. Norris and Millie too?"

"Yes. You can't get too much information on this kind of subject. We're all looking forward to it."

Peggy didn't think Norris would be looking forward to it, but she didn't say so. She went downstairs when she was dressed and let Shakespeare run in the backyard while she checked on her plants in the basement.

The little watermelons she was working on making larger were doing well. The growth pattern was the same, which was unfortunate. The new melons would never be accepted by the other members of the group fighting against world hunger.

She sighed. So far, she hadn't been able to keep all the nutrition that she'd built into the small melon in a larger version. It was discouraging.

Walter knocked on the open glass door. "I saw Shakespeare outside. I knew you must be down here. How is the work going?"

"Everything works, except for my melon. It doesn't want to be as big as everyone else wants it to be."

He put on his glasses and looked over her notes, a well-thought-of botanist in his own right. "I don't understand why they are insisting on size when they can have quantity."

"It's just part of the hunger pact we signed." She glanced at her watch. "I have to go. I have that lecture today at the university."

"I'm going to be there too." He looked at her over the top of his glasses. "I wouldn't miss it. Maybe we could ride together. You could update me on your police case."

"That works for me. Can you drive?"

"How about if I drive?" Steve was on the stairs. "You can both ride with me."

Peggy was about to turn him down. She thought about sitting shoulder-to-shoulder with Norris.

"Norris and Millie are coming together. We'll meet them there." Steve smiled. "No excuses."

"That sounds good. I wasn't trying to make up excuses not to ride with Norris and Millie," she refuted.

"Sure. Oh, right—just Norris. Let's go."

Peggy called Shakespeare into the house and left him in the basement again to keep him from getting over-excited about the roofers.

Her phone rang as she was grabbing her handbag and laptop to head out the door. It was Arnie.

"You're not going to believe what happened," he enthused. "I went to the storage place again today to fill out some forms. I thought I'd sweep up in there a little. A few pieces of paper were left behind by the thieves. I wanted to make sure I got my security deposit back. I opened the door to Unit 34, and it was all back."

Peggy smiled. "All of it?"

"As far as I can tell. It's a miracle. I think the thief felt guilty when he realized there was nothing of real value in there. I'm still shocked. Can you come over, and we'll go through everything?"

"I'd love to, Arnie, but I have a lecture in about thirty minutes. As soon as I can get away, I'll meet you there. That's wonderful about it all being returned."

"I know. I'm excited about it. I can't wait for you to get here."

"Me too. See you later." She let a long breath go, feeling as though she'd been holding it since Paul had told her what happened.

Steve held the door for Peggy as she started out. "You have a smug smile on your face. What's up?"

"Whoever took everything out of Arnie's storage unit returned it."

"That's unusual."

"Maybe it was a guilty conscience."

"Or maybe somebody looked through everything and decided there wasn't anything they wanted."

"You have a suspicious mind," she told him.

"It matches yours. That must be why we're so good together."

* * *

In the car on the way to the university, Walter asked Steve about the progress of his burglary investigation. "I read about it online. I have an interest in antique jewelry. That's what the ring is stealing, correct?"

Steve frowned at him in the rearview mirror. "Where did you read that?"

"I follow a blog that takes an interest in such things. They know all about your investigation."

"Interesting." Steve stopped at a traffic light. "We expect to make an arrest in that case soon."

"Really?" Walter leaned his head between the front seats. "The blog said you had no real leads."

"How does the blog writer know that?"

"The people who write the blog have inside sources on these cases," Walter explained. "Like they know these are the same thieves who struck this area a while back. That's their MO, right? They swoop in like birds of prey, grab all the sparklies they can, and fly back out again before anyone can catch them."

"I think it's fair to describe it that way. Your blog writer is very well informed. Maybe he'd like to come to work for me."

Walter thought that was really funny. "These people are the *watchdogs* of groups like the FBI and the CIA. They would never join up with them."

"Send me the link for that blog, will you?" Steve said. "I'd like to read it."

Walter scowled, not committing to helping the FBI by giving Steve the blog address.

The university was only a short distance from the house. They were parking in the crowded parking lot in no time. Steve took the laptop for Peggy as they went inside the lecture hall.

Already, a good-sized crowd had assembled. Peggy's poison plant lectures were well known in the Charlotte area. There seemed to be a more than average crowd of people in police uniforms. They weren't only from Charlotte either. Peggy recognized a few South Carolina uniforms and the sheriff of Stanly County.

"Good morning, Peggy." Eldon Brown worked for the university as a public relations expert. He was responsible for setting up this lecture and others that she'd given. "It looks like a good crowd today. I'm sure they're prepared to be amazed by what you have to say, as I am."

"Thank you, Eldon. I'm looking forward to it, as always."

Steve kissed her lightly on the lips. "I'm going to sit down before all the seats are taken."

Walter kissed her once on each cheek. "I'll see you after the program, Peggy."

Steve grinned at her after Walter walked away. "He's *only* a friend, right?"

"Go and find your seat." She laughed at his fake jealousy. She enjoyed his teasing.

Peggy gave her laptop to the student who would be setting up her PowerPoint presentation, and projecting it on the big screen while she was speaking. She thanked him for his help and walked to the podium.

After welcoming her audience, Peggy talked about past cases she'd worked with the Charlotte/Mecklenburg police.

Her presentation included newspaper articles and information she'd collected during the cases. This information explained from the beginning how the cases were determined to be botanical poisonings, how evidence was collected, how she came to conclusions about the types of poison used, and how it was administered.

She had twelve cases on the PowerPoint presentation. She could see Steve and Al nodding as the information was given out. Al had worked with her on some of the cases. In most of them, Steve had only participated in his attempts to keep her safe.

After she had laid out her past cases involving botanical poisons, she took questions from the audience.

Walter's hand was the first one up. "What about the case you're working on now?"

Peggy was a little annoyed that he'd asked that question, knowing she couldn't talk about most of the information on that case. "I am presently working on what appears to be a botanical poisoning, but it's too early in the investigation to be certain of that—or to discuss it in an open forum."

The sheriff of Stanly County asked a few questions about toxins in water. His county contained a large man-made lake that had at least a few drownings each year. Peggy had worked with him on a previous case in which a poisoning had been made to appear to be a drowning.

There were several botany students who had questions about how to get into Peggy's very specific field. She answered as openly as she could, explaining the six-week course she had to take in Raleigh to become a forensic botanist.

"You have to understand that there isn't a huge call for forensic botanists—but when you need one, nothing else will do." Everyone laughed at that. "The state can't afford to keep botanists on staff for this task, so most counties have a botanist they work with. You can't have my job in Mecklenburg County, but there are ninety-nine other counties that could be looking for a botanist in this field."

A master gardening group from the city of Concord had dozens of questions about poisonous plants they should tell people to stay away from. The group fielded thousands of questions from gardeners every year. One of the biggest questions pertained to plants that were poisonous to animals.

Peggy smiled as she leaned on the podium. "You know, I always think it's amazing how much more interested people are in protecting children and pets from poisonous plants than they are themselves. Last year, more adults died from ingesting poisonous plants than any other group. Mostly, this is because adults see themselves as being too smart to be poisoned. And yet, a relatively intelligent person will eat a poisonous plant just to see what it does."

The group laughed and talked amongst themselves for a moment, and then Peggy launched into a quick review of plants that were poisonous to horses, dogs, and cats. "A single red maple leaf can kill an adult horse."

She talked about specific plants that were deadly poisonous to humans as well, including azaleas, vinca, potato plants, and heartleaf philodendron.

As always during this type of presentation, there were the myths of what was, and what wasn't, poisonous. She suggested never inviting a plant into a home or garden without knowing them properly. That included knowing if they were toxic, and if so, what to do if they were accidentally ingested.

When the presentation was over, everyone got to their feet and applauded. A dozen people made for the podium area to ask Peggy personal questions. Those were the questions she hated most because invariably someone would ask how much poison it would take to kill an adult male or female. *What is the best poison to use so you don't get caught?*

For years, she'd refused to answer. She never wanted to worry about what the outcome could be from a small speck of information. She didn't change her response after this lecture. If someone was serious about harming another person, they'd have to do it without her.

She was surprised to see Paul's face there among the attendees greeting her. He brought bad news with him.

"Al has been trying to call you all morning," he said. "They had to let Ray Quick go. He has an airtight alibi for the time you were attacked at the hospital."

Bougainvillea
Beautiful bougainvillea is native to South America. It has many different names in that area of the world. It is Spanish papelillo, primavera, três-marias, sempre-lustrosa, santa-rita, ceboleiro, roseiro, roseta, riso, pataguinha, pau-de-roseira, and flor-de-papel in Brazilian Portuguese.

Chapter Twenty-one

"How is that possible?" She raised a brow at him as several other people thanked her for her lecture. "I was there. It was *definitely* Ray Quick."

Paul frowned. "The parking lot video didn't pick up his face. He has three people who swear he was on the other side of town. One of them is a minister who works with parolees. Right now, it's your word against all of theirs."

Peggy was baffled by that information. She continued smiling and thanking her audience. It didn't make any sense that someone would say that Ray was somewhere other than the hospital parking lot knocking her around, and stealing Ann Fletcher's file.

"I'm sorry, Mom. I was hoping taking him in from the Kozy Kettle would be an end to it, but he's out on the street again. Do you want me to ask Al for police protection?"

"No. Besides, how could he do that when Ray has an alibi? He'd have to have a good of reason to spend money that way."

"I wish there was something else I could do."

She leaned her head close to his. "Arnie called me. He said everything is back in the storage unit. I think that's enough for you to do in one day."

Paul smiled, and Steve walked up, wondering what was going on. "Paul. Is anything up?"

"You might as well tell him," Peggy said.

Paul related his news about Ray. Steve shook his head. "I don't see how that's possible."

"They might be working with him," Paul said. "But we couldn't hold him."

Steve took a deep breath but didn't have time to say anything before Millie and Norris joined them.

Millie Sanford smiled at Peggy as she congratulated her on a great lecture. "I'm going home to throw away all of my evil plants tonight. I'll never look at them as being helpless and harmless again."

Norris was less enthusiastic. "We learned most of that stuff in training. It was a very good lecture—from a layman's point of view."

"Thanks, Millie." Peggy glanced at her partner. "Norris."

"We have to get going," Millie told Steve. "There's been another robbery. This one is on Sharon Road. Same old story. The burglars knew the couple was out of town and took some expensive antique jewelry."

"Okay." Steve kissed Peggy, but spoke to Paul. "Are you on duty? Can you go with her today?"

"I'd like to, but Mai has a doctor's appointment. It takes forever because the doctor keeps rushing out to deliver babies as we're waiting. I could call someone."

"You don't need to call anyone," Peggy assured them. "I'm going to meet Arnie at the mini- storage, and then either to the shop or the ME's office, depending on who I hear from first."

Steve and Paul traded uncomfortable glances.

"I'd be honored to tag along with Peggy," Walter volunteered. "Excellent lecture, as always, my dear."

"Good idea." Steve clapped him on the shoulder. "Thanks."

"I have to go." Paul looked at his watch. "Mai gets hyper if we're not there on time, even if the doctor is never on time for our appointment. I hope this is the last one."

Steve dropped Peggy and Walter off at the house. He and Peggy argued all the way home from the university. Steve wanted her to take the day off and stay inside to avoid meeting up with Ray Quick again—at least until Al could figure out what was going on.

It was a losing battle for Steve, as he was fairly sure it would be. "But I had to try." He kissed her goodbye and asked her to be careful.

"She's in good hands, my man." Walter held up his umbrella like a sword. "I'll see to it that she stays safe."

Peggy let out a sigh of relief when Steve was gone. She turned to Walter and assured him that he didn't need to come to the mini-storage with her.

"I'd be letting down a friend and going back on my word if I don't accompany you, my dear. Steve knows what he's talking about since this is his line of business, as surely as you or I might know the difference between a daffodil and a jonquil."

Peggy understood the difference between being thankful to have someone who cared about her, and being obnoxious about trying to get rid of him. She insisted on driving her own car, though. At least that would make her feel somewhat in control.

Arnie was still waiting at the mini-storage. Peggy called him to come and open the gate.

He was surprised to see that she wasn't alone. The two men shook hands as they introduced themselves. The three of them drove from the parking lot to Unit 34.

"You can imagine how surprised I was to see everything back here again." Arnie used his key to unlock the door.

"What do you think happened?" Walter asked. "It seems to me that it must be someone who works here."

Arnie agreed. "The manager acted as surprised as I felt when I brought him down here. I thought he may have put all of my things into a different storage unit by accident, and when he realized what he'd done, he put it all back."

The two men congratulated each other on their theories. Peggy went inside the storage unit, thankful that they had no idea what had *really* happened. She hoped they never found out.

"Whoever was responsible did a bang-up job of putting everything back." Arnie chuckled. "It's much neater and better organized than Harry had it."

"Where are the files?" Peggy thought she should act enthusiastic about finding them, even though she knew there was nothing of any great importance in them.

"Of course." Arnie used his inhaler before picking out the two boxes that contained information about John. "I hope there's something in here that will help you find out what happened to your husband."

Walter looked around at the boxes filled with papers and other more tangible items. He picked up one of Ann Fletcher's herb books. "It looks like there was a garden enthusiast here."

Peggy joined him, and perused some of the books that contained deadly herbs and plants—including lily of the valley. "I'm afraid she may have been too enthusiastic about her reading material. It may have caused her death."

She thought about the woman who was on the slab at the morgue. As soon as the tissue samples came back, they'd know if she died from convallatoxin. Peggy wondered if the two women were close.

"Here is the information about my sister that Harry gathered together through the years." Arnie put two more boxes at her feet. "Have you found anything out of the ordinary by exhuming her?"

"It's too soon to tell. I'm sorry. As soon as I know something definitive, I'll let you know."

"I brought a small cart so we could take these records someplace else to look at them," Arnie said. "I don't know what all is in them, but I hope they'll make a difference."

"Look at this," Walter said from the other side of the storage shed, behind an old rocking chair. "There must be a small fortune in jewelry here. What do you think, Peggy?"

Peggy and Arnie went to examine the find. There were several pieces of very good antique jewelry.

"I'm no jewelry appraiser," Peggy said. "But these stones look like the real thing to me."

Walter sank his teeth into one of the gold settings around the jewels. "I believe this is real too. As I said—a lot of old jewelry that must be worth a small fortune."

"I don't believe Ann ever owned anything like this." Arnie shook his head. "She and Harry barely got by. They were always borrowing money. I can't imagine where this came from."

The three sifted through the rest of the boxes in the storage unit, but there was no other jewelry. The box that had held the jewels was filled with personal items that had once been Ann's. Nothing of any real worth was there—a hairbrush, some old photos, and a few other trinkets.

"I think we should bring this box too," Peggy said. "It may have something to do with why Ann was killed."

It was something in her own thoughts from hearing Steve talk about the antique jewelry thefts around Charlotte. The other items in the box with the jewelry were at least twenty years old. Steve had mentioned that a similar occurrence had happened in the past. She wondered how far past. Was it possible Harry had been involved in that previous ring of thieves, and Ann had paid the price for it?

Between them, they got the five boxes moved to Peggy's car. The facility manager rode by on his golf cart, asking if everything was okay, but he didn't offer to help. Peggy was surprised that Arnie wanted her to take the boxes of files that pertained to Ann's death as well as the other three.

"I'm staying at a motel," he said. "You have a permanent place you can keep them, and we can look through them. Seems like the best solution."

"I don't mind at all," she replied. "And I have an alarm system to protect them."

Walter nodded. "Not to mention a large husband who is in the FBI, and a beast of a dog who would attack first and ask questions later. These items are as safe at her house as they would be in Fort Knox."

Peggy laughed at that. Her phone buzzed. It was a text from Dorothy. There was new information. "Why don't you come for dinner, Arnie? We can look through the boxes afterward. I have to meet with the medical examiner."

He agreed. "Do you need any help with the boxes?"

"No. I have to drop off Walter first anyway. We can get them into the house before I go."

"All right then. I'll meet you at your place for dinner." He smiled. "Except that I don't know where your place is."

Peggy took his phone, put in her address and phone number in his contacts. "Let's say seven, okay? My large, FBI husband will probably be there too. Definitely my dog, Shakespeare, will be. See you then, Arnie."

Walter and Peggy left the mini-storage. She saw Arnie

in his white Cadillac coming up behind them.

"So you think Harry Fletcher was involved in the jewelry heist from years ago?" Walter asked in an excited voice. "That would mean the jewelry has been stored away with no one realizing it all these years. Are you going to tell Steve?"

"Later. When I see him. Right now, I have to deal with whatever Dorothy has found out, and then I have to spend some time at The Potting Shed. We'll have to be patient and wait for answers."

"I could email some pictures of the jewelry to my friend at the conspiracy blog and see what he thinks," Walter offered.

"I don't think that's a good idea since it could be involved in a murder and this burglary ring that the FBI is looking into. Not unless you want some unfriendly faces with badges knocking on your door tonight."

"Oh, heavens no," Walter retorted. "Not that I'm afraid of the FBI, or your husband. I was just saying that so Arnie would feel safe. May I join you for dinner, and the after party of snooping through those boxes?"

"Absolutely. I'm sure we could use another pair of eyes." Peggy maneuvered through the light traffic until she reached her house. "Besides, you deserve it after being my babysitter and helping me lug these boxes around."

"I wouldn't have missed it!"

Walter had the opportunity to prove his worth on the subject as they struggled to take the boxes into Peggy's house. The roofers were taking a break from their labors, sitting under a magnolia tree in the shade, watching as they walked back and forth from the kitchen door to the car.

When everything was inside—and Shakespeare had gone for a quick run in the back of the house—Peggy locked up and was ready to go. Walter was sitting in the car, waiting for her.

"You can't come with me to the ME's office," she told

him as she got in the car.

"I promised Steve I'd stay with you. Besides, I'd love to hear what the medical examiner has learned in this case of yours."

"That's the problem. It's too hot for you to wait in the car. You can't come into the building." She fudged a little on that, but he couldn't attend the meeting. "I'll let you know what happens. That's the best I can do. Steve will understand."

Walter considered his words. "If you're certain. I don't want to get on the FBI's bad list."

"I'm certain. The parking lot is right beside the building, and there's security. I'm not worried about it." She didn't mention that this was the parking lot where her car was vandalized.

"Then I'll see you later, Peggy. If you have any problems at all, please call me. I can be there quickly and roust the ruffians."

She smiled and thanked him. "I'll do that." She wasn't sure he could find the morgue or how long it would take him to get there with the way he drove. "Seven sharp for dinner."

He bowed slightly. "It shall be my honor."

* * *

Peggy parked close to the building when she arrived at the medical examiner's office. She'd had to turn her phone off to get there. Dorothy kept texting and calling her. Peggy didn't like to talk on her phone when she was driving.

Tom saluted her as she passed through the metal detector. She made small talk with him until her handbag came through the detector, and then she hurried toward Dorothy's office.

Dorothy wasn't there, of course. One of the interns told her that Dorothy was waiting in the conference room with a few other visitors. Peggy took off her suit coat and left it at her desk before joining them. She wished she could step out of her shoes too. They were pinching her toes.

She opened the door to the conference room. Al was there, and so was Norris. She wondered where Steve and Millie were. Why were *any* of them there? They hadn't heard about the jewelry she'd found as yet.

Dorothy got up nervously from her chair. "Dr. Lee, at last. We've been waiting for you."

"Sorry." Peggy smiled at Al. "I had an errand to run after the lecture this morning."

"Take a chair," Dorothy said. "I only want to go over our findings once so I invited a few people who might have an interest in Ann Fletcher's death."

Peggy itched to ask why the FBI had an interest. Was it something Dorothy had found out?

"First of all, thank you for coming, Detective McDonald and Agent Rankin. Let's get down to the case." Dorothy had put together a slideshow that revealed details about the dead woman and the tests performed on her.

"As you can see, the corpse was in good condition considering the length of time she's been buried. We immediately tested her for convallatoxin, which at this time could only be found in her tissues. She tested off the charts for the poison, although our tests also revealed that it was not a rapid death, but one that took place over a period of time."

Peggy's cell phone rang. She opted to apologize and put it on mute. She could see it was Selena. Whatever it was would have to wait.

Norris glared at her and changed position in his chair. "Not sure why I'm here, Dr. Beck. This seems to be a *local* problem."

Dorothy smiled. "I'm getting to that, Agent Rankin."

"Please proceed," Al said.

"Thank you." Dorothy cleared her throat and changed

the slide they were looking at. "We learned quickly that this corpse may have been buried as Ann Fletcher, but the body tells us another story. I was able to verify from hospital records that this woman *wasn't* Ann Fletcher. I learned an hour ago that her name was Sheila Conway. As you can see from the photos of the two women, they looked a lot alike. But we verified this information with fingerprints and other records."

Norris sat forward in his chair, a sudden look of anticipation on his face. "I recognize that name."

Dorothy nodded. "That's why you're here, Agent. Miss Conway was a suspect in a series of jewelry thefts that plagued Charlotte for a year. I believe several members of that group were arrested, but a few more were never found."

"Including the ringmaster," Norris said. "We know from the work done at that time that the agents involved had reason to believe the leader was a woman."

"I read that in the files," Dorothy said. "It appears we may have found the leader of that group."

Al shuffled through some papers Dorothy had given him on the case. "So you think this Sheila Conway was poisoned by the group and then buried in place of Ann Fletcher. But where is Mrs. Fletcher?"

"I have to go." Norris sprang to his feet, grabbed his paperwork, and ran out the door.

Dorothy tapped her pencil on the table. "That was rude."

Peggy shrugged. "Tell me about it."

They forgot about Norris as they discussed all the findings they'd had for Sheila Conway's body.

Al wasn't sure how the two cases related, except that the wrong woman was in Ann Fletcher's grave. "We'll be following up on this, trying to figure out if there was a connection between them or if this was a random mistake."

Dorothy looked at Al over the top of her glasses. "I hardly think this was random, Al. I think someone did this on purpose."

Peggy agreed with her. She knew Al liked to be thorough. That was good, but it seemed to her that the evidence was staring them in the face.

She also had the feeling that Norris knew something more that he wasn't telling them. She didn't think he left so abruptly for no reason.

When the meeting was over, Peggy went into the hall and called Steve. Normally she wouldn't call him about something either of them were working on, but she had information to trade that might help her understand Norris's actions.

"Hi Peggy," Steve said. "Why am I not surprised to hear from you?"

She rolled her eyes. "Because Norris told you that our cases have suddenly meshed?"

"Very perceptive. What do you need?"

"Actually, I might have something *you* need. I'm leaving here in a few minutes. Can you meet me at The Potting Shed?"

"I can be there in about thirty minutes."

"See you then."

Dorothy was waiting for her when she got off the phone. "You had the same feeling I did, right? Agent Rankin knew something and didn't want to share."

Peggy nodded. "It seems to me that if Sheila Conway was somehow implicated in the jewelry thefts twenty years ago, and now we find her in Ann Fletcher's grave, it's a good guess that she was there to distract people from Ann Fletcher."

"That's what I thought. I wonder why Al didn't think the same thing?"

"Maybe he did, and he didn't want to share either."

"What's the point of having meetings together if we're the only ones sharing information?"

"I don't know. But I'm hoping I can get a few hints from my husband." Peggy smiled.

"Good idea. Maybe that's the only way we're going to stay in the loop." Dorothy glanced at her watch. "I'm putting some extra people on the case to find out if Ann Fletcher is dead. That seems like an important hurdle to me. Let me know what Steve has to say about everything."

Peggy promised that she would keep her updated and left the building. Trying to keep her promise to be more careful, she peeked out into the parking lot before she went outside. Her car was unmolested, and she didn't see Ray Quick or any other threatening figures.

"I've been keeping an eye on things out there." Tom noticed her furtive movements. "I was embarrassed that vandalism happened on my watch. I haven't seen anything unusual."

"Thanks, Tom."

"I can walk out to your car with you, if you like."

"I think I'll be okay. I appreciate the offer." Peggy smiled at him as she opened the door and went outside. She winced as a blast of hot, humid air hit her. Thank goodness for air conditioning.

Traffic was light as she drove to the shop and parked in the back next to the loading dock. Peggy locked her car doors and went inside. The Potting Shed truck wasn't there, so she knew Sam was out working.

She felt bad knowing that he wasn't there. Maybe Selena's call *was* an emergency. She would've worried more if it had been Sam calling, but Selena sometimes called about silly things—like large spiders and not being able to find the lizard in the pond. Thank goodness that most of the time she was perfectly capable.

In this case, Peggy walked through the back of the shop to find Selena rocking in her chair with an iced mocha in her hand. "You called?"

Selena jumped and dropped her mocha. She was quick to pick it up so only a few drops spilled. "I didn't mean you had to come over! There was a question I couldn't answer about tulips. Mrs. Eisenhower wanted to know if you had any white tulips with purple edges. I looked in the catalog and didn't see any. I thought you might know."

Peggy shook her head. "That doesn't qualify as an emergency."

"I know. You didn't have to come in to answer."

"Let's go with things that aren't an emergency as texts, and emergencies are phone calls."

"I didn't want Mrs. Eisenhower to go away unhappy. That's what you always say."

"And that's true. I'll see what I can find and get back with her. Thanks." Peggy went behind the counter to stow her bag. "Anything else interesting this morning?"

"Nope. A person called about a huge piece of corn he grew. I think he saw the watermelon story in the paper today. Now we're going to be the place to take large fruits and vegetables."

"Oh. That came out today? Did we get a copy?"

"Of course." Selena reached around her and produced the gardening section of the paper. "I think we should have taken out an ad at the same time."

Peggy read the story and smiled at the picture of her, Dorian Hubbard, and the large watermelon. "You're probably right. Still, they mentioned our address and phone number. That was good."

Selena shrugged and went back to drinking her mocha. "What have you been up to today?"

Before Peggy could answer, Steve came in from the back of the shop.

"I know you're busy," she said to him. "I'll get what I

wanted to show you out of the car."

"I'm not *that* busy." He smiled. "Let's go over to the Kozy Kettle and get some coffee. You can show me what you have after you tell me."

"That sounds wonderful."

"What about me?" Selena asked. "If you two go over there, I won't get to hear the good stuff."

"Hello, Selena." Steve said to her. "I'm sure Peggy can fill you in later. Thanks for watching the store."

Peggy thanked her too, but Selena was determined to be cranky about it. Peggy might have felt worse if she didn't know that her assistant already had a break that morning, and the shop wasn't busy.

"Are you sure you want to go over there?" Peggy asked Steve when they were in the sunny courtyard.

"I know how Emil and Sofia feel about me." Steve took her hand in his. "I can live with it."

Peggy felt her friends' eyes on them as soon as they walked in. It didn't help that it was a slow time for the coffee shop. That gave them plenty of time to hover.

Steve got coffee and a bagel. Peggy just got peach tea. They sat at a table inside. The occasional grunt from Emil made them realize that he was listening to their conversation. Once they had their order, Peggy decided they should sit outside.

There was a beautiful bougainvillea blooming beside their table. The huge red and purple flowers danced in the light breeze, and drooped down from the pretty green pot where Sofia had planted it.

"So? What are we talking about?" Steve asked.

"I got the boxes of files from Arnie this morning. I also took another box of personal items that Harry had stored there. Arnie thinks the items belonged to Ann." She sipped her tea. "There were some very valuable pieces of antique jewelry that probably didn't belong to her. Arnie said she and Harry never owned much and were always borrowing money."

"You've heard that there was another antique jewelry burglary ring in Charlotte about twenty years ago," he guessed as he spread cream cheese on his bagel. "Sometimes I wonder why you're not working for me."

"Because I like you too much to let that happen." She grinned at him and snatched a bit of his bagel. "Do you have records of the jewelry that was taken back then that we could compare it too?"

He nodded. "Of course. This is the FBI. We're all about records."

"Good. Then we can trade. I'd like to know why Agent Norris lit up like a Christmas tree this morning at the medical examiner's meeting."

Dahlia
The dahlia is the national flower of Mexico. The mountains of Mexico and Guatemala are the home of this beautiful and versatile flower. Spanish conquistadors, in the 16th century, brought back a vast collection of plants. The hollow stems of these plants were many times more than twenty-feet high and used for hauling water to the city. The Aztec name for dahlias was acocotli, or water-cane.

Chapter Twenty-two

Steve laughed. "He called me as soon as he left the room. It sounds like Ann and Harry Fletcher may have killed this young woman whose body you exhumed—at least that's the way Norris heard it. What did you think?"

"It could go that way. He said Sheila Conway's name might have been mentioned in the older robbery. I suppose Ann could have faked her own death by killing Sheila. From her reading material, she may have been able to poison Sheila with lily of the valley. Does that mean you see Ann as being the head of the burglary ring?"

"I'm not sure what's going on *today*, but it's possible she was part of what happened twenty years ago."

"Does Norris think the same people are involved in the new burglaries?" she questioned.

"He does. He may be right. It looks like it could be an operation that has been moving around the country for years, possibly stealing millions of dollars in antique jewelry."

Peggy sipped her tea, not sure what to make of those

ideas. "You're welcome to look at what I have. Do you think that means that Harry was part of the robberies?"

Steve covered Peggy's hand with his on the sun-warmed table. "Not necessarily. In fact, he may have been murdered because he could identify Ann. He might have been involved in the past, but Ann may not have clued him in to what was going on now."

She nodded. "Otherwise, he wouldn't have been crusading to find out who killed her, right?"

"Pretty much." He finished his coffee, and leaned toward her. "Stay away from this, Peggy. It might get a lot more dangerous now that Ann has been exposed. She might think you know more than you do. It may have been her that sent Ray Quick after you."

"I'll do what I can to stay out of it, but Dorothy is counting on me to finish the investigation."

"Okay. Just don't do anything that might attract more attention to you."

"I won't. Do you want to see the jewelry now?"

"What about the files you got on John?" His brown eyes were steady on hers.

"There isn't much information there. I don't know if Harry just wanted my help with Ann's death, or if he really thought what he had would make a difference."

"I'm sorry. Would you like me to look through them?"

"Maybe so, after all of this is over. Thanks."

They got up to leave. Steve waved to Emil and Sofia, who were standing with their noses pressed against the glass behind them. Emil almost tripped over a chair trying to pretend he wasn't watching them. Sofia crossed herself several times and turned away.

"Why don't they like me?" Steve asked.

She laughed at the question. "They think you're a bad husband because you don't spend all your time with me. I think it's also because they want to hook me up with someone from their family who needs a wife."

"I guess I can see that—as long as Emil doesn't have his eye on you."

They were both laughing at that as they walked back into The Potting Shed. Selena was playing games on her tablet and looked up as they came in.

"So do I get to hear the good stuff now?" she asked.

"Later," Peggy told her. "I'll be right back."

Steve walked out to the car with her. She showed him the jewelry she was talking about and put the pieces into a cloth bag for him.

"You'll let me know what happens." She smiled and kissed him.

"Yes. Thank you for your cooperation." He put his arms around her. "I'm thinking about making you my confidential informant."

"That sounds sexy. I think I'd like that."

"It's as good as done."

They kissed again as Sam pulled The Potting Shed truck beside Peggy's car. "Hey, don't we have some kind of rule about people not doing that kind of thing in the parking lot? If not, I think we should write one. It gives the place a bad reputation."

Sam and Steve shook hands and exchanged a few words. Steve thanked him for going places with Peggy so she didn't have to go alone and then he had to leave.

"How is the Drummond job going?" Peggy asked Sam after she waved goodbye to Steve.

"Great. I like working with Claire. She's wide open to anything. I think the blueberry bushes are going to be a hit. We're going to make a pile of money on her yard, and she's going to recommend us to all her friends."

"Excellent. I'm glad you two are finally able to work on a project together.'

They went into the shop as Selena was having a

conversation with a short man in a gray suit. Sam retreated to the back storage area.

Peggy smiled as she greeted her customer. "I was wondering when you were going to show up!"

"You knew I'd be here." He hugged her. "So where are my fabulous dahlias that you promised to set aside for me?"

"Blackberry Ripple, if I remember correctly, TJ?" She started toward the orders she'd put aside for him.

He rubbed his hands together. "Yes! I'm looking forward to having them in my yard after seeing them at the Festival of Flowers this year."

"I also added some Raspberry Sherbet dahlias with them." Peggy held out the bag for him. "I think the combination will be spectacular together."

"I can't wait until they bloom next year. I'll invite you for tea." He kissed her cheek. "I saw you in the newspaper today. It was a very good picture. I hope it doesn't make The Potting Shed *too* famous. I don't want to have to fight my way in the door."

"I don't think you have to worry about that, but we all have to stay in business, don't we?"

"I certainly hope *you* do, Peggy. I'll see you later." The small man tipped his gray cap to Selena and left.

"Why do they make flowers sound like food?" Selena asked.

"They don't—not all the time. Sometimes they're named after famous people or famous places. The colorful food names are cute. And someone has to name new species every year. I think they do the best they can."

Selena went back to her games—Peggy didn't mind when they weren't busy.

Peggy spent some time working on the small pond in the shop. Seasons didn't seem to matter much when plants were kept indoors all the time. Her purple water irises were about to bloom. Some clearing of the root system for all the plants was in order.

Customers came and went as she worked. A small lizard kept watch over her activities, darting away if she got too close. Most of The Potting Shed customers were comfortable talking to Selena. Peggy always greeted them, and many sat down for a while to pick her brain about one garden problem or another. She answered questions about everything from cutting back roses to getting rid of voles.

She really loved this part of owning the garden shop. Talking with other gardeners about their problems and successes was special to her. Seeing friends come and go with her flowers in their hands made her day. She wanted the shop to succeed so she could continue, but no amount of money could make her feel any better about what she did.

The forensic work was challenging and exciting. She liked it too. Between the two things, she was well satisfied with her career.

After lunch with Sam and Selena, Peggy was looking through fall catalogues for new products, as she always did. Arnie called her. He sounded nervous, maybe even a little afraid.

"Peggy? Someone showed up at the storage unit a few minutes ago. He said his name is Ray Quick and that Ann had something that belonged to him. Have you done anything with that box of stuff I let you have today?"

"No," she lied, wanting to hear more about what Ray wanted. "What is he looking for?"

"He says he's looking for that jewelry we found. He says it belongs to him and that Ann was supposed to leave it for him, but Harry took it with everything else."

She was beginning to get a bad feeling about this. "Where are you, Arnie?"

"I think I'm in trouble, Peggy." The phone went dead before he could say where he was.

* * *

Peggy drove to Arnie's motel room. The door was locked, and there was no response when she knocked. She convinced the motel manager that she was Arnie's wife, and he opened the door for her.

When the manager was gone—after a warning about two of them staying in the room that was meant for a single—Peggy started looking around for some idea of where he could be. She tried his cell phone again. There was no answer. Thinking about how Harry had died made her nervous. What if Ray Quick wanted to kill Arnie too?

If Ann was still alive, and had killed her husband because he could recognize her, would she hold back because Arnie was her brother?

The only other place she could imagine Arnie and Ray going was the mini-storage. She got back in the car and headed that way. She took a few minutes to call Al and let him know what was going on.

"All he said was that he *could* be in trouble, right?" Al asked as though he was only half listening.

"Yes, but I'm afraid he might be headed in the same direction as Harry."

"I can't get away right now, Peggy, but I'll send an officer to the mini-storage to assist you. We've been following the trail of breadcrumbs left behind by Sheila Conway. I think it's possible that she was the head of the old burglary ring. I still can't explain why she was buried under Ann Fletcher's name, but things of that nature happen sometimes."

"So you don't think Ann might still be alive and head of the new burglary ring?"

"I don't know yet. That irritating agent of Steve's has been here to pick up everything we had on the burglaries twenty years ago. I hope his theory is correct just so he stays out of my office. What does Steve see in him anyway?"

"I don't know if Steve likes him or not, but he says he gets the job done." Peggy made the turn into the mini-storage. "I have to figure out how to get in here without a passcode, Al. Thanks for sending a car."

"Peggy, don't do anything until my officer gets there, you hear? Peggy?"

"Sorry, Al. There's bad reception out here." She scraped her fingernails across her phone. "Talk to you later."

If she was right—and Arnie was Ray Quick's next target—she couldn't wait for the Charlotte/Mecklenburg police officer to arrive. She locked her car and went as quickly as she could to the office of the storage facility.

Of course, the same man she'd met before was on-duty. He took one look at her and immediately got to his feet. "I don't want to see you here. Leave now, and I won't call the police."

"You don't have to call the police—they're already on the way." She took out her pass to the medical examiner's office. "I work with the police. We have to go to Unit 34. A man's life might be in danger. I know you don't want the publicity from someone dying here."

His eyes narrowed, but he made no move toward the door. "You'd say anything to get into that unit, wouldn't you? What's so special about it? Did you know everything in there was stolen, and put back again? I need to see a search warrant if you want me to open that door without the owner's permission."

"I'm telling you—the man who owns the unit—Arnie Houck—could be dead or dying in there right now." Her sharp green eyes pinned him to the wall. "If you don't want to have TV news out here tonight, not to mention living with your own conscience, you'll open that door right now."

He got his keys from the desk. "You're crazy, you know that? If I don't find Mr. Houck in that unit, I'm having you arrested again."

"Whatever. Stop talking and let's go!"

They went quickly out to the golf cart. The manager drove haphazardly in the narrow aisles between the buildings until they came to Unit 34. Peggy snatched the keys from him, despite his loud protest, and ran to open the door.

Arnie slid out, almost into her arms. He was unconscious. His breathing was shallow, and his heartbeat was slow. It seemed as though he'd been propped up right inside the door.

"Okay." The manager ran a hand through his dark hair. "I guess you were right. What do we do now?"

Peggy had him help her lay Arnie on the pavement. "Call for an ambulance. He's been poisoned."

He shook his head, but did as he was told. "That's right. She said he was poisoned. She's from the ME's office. How the hell should I know if she knows what she's talking about?"

Peggy made Arnie as comfortable as she could. They would have to get it out of his system by the use of charcoal and hope they got to him in time. It was possible he could need blood dialysis if it had gone on too long.

His face was ashen, and he was cold. She looked at the back of his neck and found a single red mark that showed the poison had been injected in the same way it had with Harry.

Knowing now that this seemed to be about the jewelry they'd found, she called Steve to let him know. He didn't answer, but she left him a short voicemail. She didn't know if Ray and Ann would be brazen enough to tackle the FBI, but better safe than sorry. It seemed clear to her now that

Ann was involved, as she had been twenty years before. Why else kill these two men? And how else would she know about the jewelry?

The ambulance arrived at the same time as the police. Peggy made sure the paramedics understood the type of poison that was used, and that it had been injected. Many times, knowing the poison could mean the difference between life and death. There were dozens of poisons that presented in the same way as convallatoxin. She signed a document declaring that she was a poison expert, and with the medical examiner's office, when the paramedic seemed unsure of her diagnosis.

It seemed to take forever before Arnie was in the ambulance and the vehicle was leaving the mini-storage. Every moment could make the difference in his survival.

The storage manager was talking to the police officer outside the unit. Peggy went inside, and switched on the overhead light. She hoped there was some trace of Ray Quick left behind that the police could use to find him. She was furious at him, popping in and out to threaten and kill people. They had to put an end to it.

From the look of it, Arnie and Ray had wrestled through the boxes in the storage building. The floor was filled with debris. Boxes were turned on their sides, and nothing was where she'd last seen it. She was so glad she'd already taken the boxes that had John's files and the information Harry had collected about his wife's death. At least they were safe.

How surprised Harry would be to know that Ann was still alive after all these years. She wondered if he'd actually seen her before he was killed.

There was a cell phone on the floor. It seemed so out of place amidst the older items. Peggy picked it up carefully with a piece of paper and looked at it. When she pushed the button, she knew at once that it didn't belong to Arnie. Ray Quick had dropped his cell phone. But was it an accident, or was it a trap?

Sunflower
The sunflower has been a source of joy and inspiration for artists for hundreds of years. They have been native to the Americas since 1000 B.C., where they were cultivated as a valuable food source. The bright flower with the happy face was brought to new areas, and their popularity grew worldwide. Their meanings include loyalty and longevity, vibrancy and energy. It's not unusual to see them as part of bridal bouquets.

Chapter Twenty-three

Peggy jumped when the phone in her hand rang. She wasn't sure if she should answer it or leave it alone. When she'd thought about it, she pressed the talk button. "Yes?"

"Dr. Lee." It was a woman's voice.

"Ann Fletcher?"

"That's right. I suppose it was an easy guess when I wasn't where I was supposed to be."

"You could say that."

"I heard your lecture on botanical poisons. You're much more knowledgeable about such things than I am. I enjoy playing around with them, but my real knowledge is limited."

"Too busy robbing people of their antique jewelry, no doubt."

Ann's laugh was husky. "I suppose so. I've found it much more lucrative than knowing about poison plants. And really, I only need to know *one*. It does everything I want it to."

"I don't find talking about killing people with

convallatoxin particularly amusing. I'm going to hang up now, and give this phone to the police."

"Cool! I'll just drop the one in my hand into a trashcan on my way out of town. Nice talking with you, Peggy."

She's going to get away again. Peggy didn't want that to happen. "I thought you wanted the jewelry you left behind."

"Are you offering it?"

Peggy thought fast. "As you said, the botanical poison information isn't worth much money. I have the jewelry. It looks quite expensive. I thought I might sell it—unless it's worth more to you for some sentimental reason."

"Interesting. So you're shaking me down *not* to give that stuff to the police?"

"I work for the medical examiner part-time. I don't really feel the need to share the jewelry with the police. I think I could make enough pawning it to pay off some bills. What do you think?"

Peggy knew she was playing a dangerous game with Ann, but she was the only one who could play it. Steve or Al were both too much a part of the system. Peggy had only been part of the situation because of Harry and Arnie. Would Ann fall for it?

"If you're serious about only wanting the money, maybe we can come to some kind of an arrangement. What did you have in mind?"

"I'm not really sure." Peggy searched her brain. "I thought it might be more valuable to you because the pieces *could* have your DNA on them. The pieces were already valuable, or you wouldn't have stolen them. I only need one-hundred-thousand dollars to pay off my debts. Is that unreasonable?"

"That actually sounds quite fair," Ann said. "Keep this phone. I'll call you as soon as I can set something up. I'm looking forward to doing business with you, Peggy."

The phone went dead, and Peggy took in a huge gulp of air. What was she thinking? Steve and Al would both hit the ceiling when she told them what she'd done.

On the other hand, Ann was about to leave Charlotte again—with at least one person's death behind her—she didn't know about Arnie yet. There could be others, like Sheila Conway, that she'd killed through the years.

The police could look around all they liked, as Al had told her—accidents happened all the time. They might never prove that Ann had killed Sheila so she could disappear. That would leave Harry's death unsolved.

Peggy couldn't let her walk away this time. She wanted to stop Ann from ever coming back to Charlotte again. The only way to do that seemed to be catching her red-handed.

Her mind was buzzing with possibilities as she walked back to her car in the parking lot. Maybe they could make the exchange somewhere—the money for the jewelry—and Al could catch Ann then. Or Steve. She didn't care which part of law enforcement did it. They could fight about it later.

She got to her car just as her cell phone rang. "Hello. I guess you got my message."

"I did," Steve agreed. "What's going on?"

Peggy explained what had happened to Arnie and her phone call with Ann. "She's going to leave again, and you might never catch her. This way, we could set something up so that when she brings me the money, you could take her down."

"That's not going to happen. Even saying we know about what you're doing, screw-ups happen all the time. I don't want to risk your life."

"This is probably the only way, Steve. Be reasonable. If you don't want to do this for the burglaries, Al will want to do it for the murders."

"I'll talk to Al. We'll find some other way. Go home, Peggy, or go to the garden shop. You'll be safe there while we thrash all of this out."

"I'm on my way back to The Potting Shed right now. I'll talk to you later."

Peggy really planned to go to the shop, but she got a call from Dorothy that took her to the ME's office. She called Selena and let her know that she'd be closing that evening. She'd probably head home after what Dorothy had to say.

She parked and went inside, thinking about Arnie, and wondering if he was okay. She called the hospital, but there was no word on his status yet. Dorothy was in her office with news about Sheila's body.

"Her tissue samples tested positive for convallatoxin. I'd say it came from the same source as what killed Harry Fletcher, but I'm not an expert."

Peggy sat down. "The source could be traced, but I have no doubt there would have to be two sources with the length of time between their deaths. The toxin would become weaker as it was stored. And I think the lady who killed both of them enjoys making a new batch every so often."

Dorothy sucked in her breath. "You *talked* to her? Is it Ann Fletcher?"

Peggy explained everything to her. The office was closing down for the night, and employees stopped by to say goodnight as they talked. Peggy also explained her plan for putting Ann in jail for the murders.

"What a great idea. Do you think the police will go for it?" Dorothy asked.

"Al might, but Steve is going to be a pain in the butt about it. You'd think I'd never done anything like this before. " Peggy rolled her eyes and sighed.

"But it's nice that he cares, right? Wouldn't you hate it if he set you up all the time without a thought for your life? I don't think I'd like that very much."

Peggy smiled. "You're right. I'm glad he loves me. But sometimes I feel like he wants an orchid instead of a sunflower, you know?"

Dorothy laughed until she had tears in her eyes. "What a novel way to say it! Leave it to you to find a plant reference."

"I suppose so."

"I'm going home. I hope you are too. We'll deal with this tomorrow, I'm sure." Dorothy grabbed her handbag. "Do you need a ride home?"

"No. Thanks. I have the car. I'll see you tomorrow."

Peggy went to her desk and watered the plants that were there. She'd also made it her responsibility to make sure all the plants in the office were taken care of, when she was working. There was a very pretty prayer plant that was leaning toward one of the windows. She watered it carefully and turned the pot so it would start leaning the other way as it sought the sun.

She'd just picked up her bag when the cell phone rang. Her hands shook a tiny bit as she realized it was *Ray's* cell phone that was ringing.

"Hi, Peggy." It was Ann again. "I have everything set up on my end for the swap. Are you ready?"

"I just have to pick up the jewelry, and I'll be ready." *And call Steve and Al.* Neither one of them were going to be happy with this short notice.

"Great. Drive over to Panther's Stadium. It's a little crazy right now because they're working on renovations, but I think it will be a great place to meet."

"Sounds good to me."

"And Peggy? Don't bring reinforcements. Ray just picked up your daughter-in-law—the one with the big belly. I'd hate for anything to happen to her. What sort of

effect do you think an overdose of convallatoxin would
have on a fetus? See you soon."

Spiraea
*Native to the U.S., spiraea tomentosa is a tall,
perennial shrub usually found in wetlands. Native
Americans used the flowers and leaves to treat diarrhea,
dysentery, and morning sickness.*

Chapter Twenty-four

It wasn't a difficult decision to make. Normally, she
would have gone alone to meet Ann. It was her way. It
wasn't that she wasn't afraid, it was just better to get it
done like that and not endanger anyone else.

But all of that had changed knowing that Ann had Mai.
Just the idea that Ann *knew* about Mai was enough to cause
a shiver to go down her spine.

Ann could be bluffing. Mai could be sitting at home,
waiting for Paul. She might be happily involved with a box
of donuts and some milk.

Peggy knew she couldn't take that chance. She wasn't
sure how to find out if Ann was bluffing without telling
Paul about the situation. She tried Mai's cell phone—there
was no response. She hoped that was a good thing. She
didn't have time to get the jewelry together and check on
Mai.

She was going to have to involve others in this
situation.

Steve and Al both answered their phones when she

called. She suggested a brief meeting somewhere safe, away from prying eyes. Al said they should meet at her house where it wouldn't look as though they were converging on the place.

Steve agreed. "I'll bring the jewelry with me. Be careful, Peggy. This could be out of control very easily."

"Should we tell Paul?" she asked.

"I don't think so. If he knew, he'd be too emotional to be any good to us. We can't meet Ann Fletcher with guns blazing. We have to let this play out, and then take her."

Those were the same thoughts running through Peggy's head. She hated not to tell her son—he was bound to find out at some time—then he'd be angry. But she agreed to Steve's idea, got in her car, and drove home.

If Ray Quick, or any of Ann's thugs were following her on the way home, Peggy couldn't tell. She looked at the cars going up and down Queens Road. Any of them could be watching her. She was glad that she'd invited Al and Steve to help her.

Steve was already at the house when she arrived. She went in, scared and shaky. Even Shakespeare was subdued. He whined and nuzzled her hand instead of barking and jumping. His big brown eyes looked nervous.

"There you are." Steve put his arms around her and held her tight. "Are you okay?"

"I can't believe she knew enough about me to grab Mai. That's the worst of it. Is there any way to tell if Ann's lying? I know we can't say anything to Paul. I tried calling Mai, but she didn't pick up."

"I sent Millie over—dressed like a cable repairman. She said the house was empty. There was no sign of a struggle."

"I imagine Mai went along quietly for the baby's sake." Peggy shook her head, tears starting to her green eyes. "I'll never forgive myself if something happens to her or the baby."

"This wasn't your fault," he said. "They were the ones who got physical with you. You were just doing your job. You didn't know all of this was involved."

"I wish that made me feel better."

Al knocked on the kitchen door and then came quickly inside. "I don't think anyone is watching the house."

"I don't think so either," Steve agreed. "I have Norris and two other agents keeping an eye on things."

"I have a few officers out there too." Al grinned. "Looks like we're pretty secure here. Do you have the jewelry?"

"I brought it with me. I wish we were making the trade here. Panther's Stadium is a large, open area, not to mention the mess from the renovations. Any ideas?" Steve asked.

"I guess we'll set up a perimeter and let Peggy walk in with the jewelry. Surely with my guys and your team, she should be safe."

"What about Mai?" Peggy asked. "She's very pregnant. The baby could come at any time."

"Let's hope she holds off for a while."

Steve put his arm around her. "You don't have to do this. We know where to find Ann and her crew now. We can do this without you,"

"I wouldn't take that kind of chance with Mai's life," she said. "I'll be okay. You two just lay low enough that you can come in quickly if there's trouble. I can handle the rest."

"You don't have to worry about that," Al assured her. "You know we've got your back. Just don't try any fancy moves in there. We want you and Mai out safely."

"That's all I have in mind."

The kitchen door opened again. Paul walked in with a concerned expression on his face. "I was on my way home and saw all the lights on—not to mention the police up and down the street. What's up? Did something else happen, Mom?"

Peggy couldn't look into his eyes and lie to him, even if it was for the best. "There's a problem. You should probably sit down."

* * *

Paul took the news much better than they had expected. He was upset, but his training stood him well. "Are we just sitting here talking about what to do, or is there a plan?"

Steve put his hand on Paul's shoulder. "There's a plan, but you're not going to be part of it."

"Like hell I'm not." He glared at Steve. "You're sending my *mother* into harm's way to rescue my *wife and daughter*. Try to keep me away."

Al shook his head and shrugged. "The boy's got a point, Steve. He's one of the best officers I've ever seen— except maybe for me and his father. He can handle this."

Steve reluctantly agreed. "All right. We're set to do this. Peggy has to go there alone. We'll follow with our people behind us. Paul, you'll come with us."

The plan was simple, but so much could go wrong. Peggy realized that as she got in the car with the antique jewelry in her handbag and headed toward the stadium.

She wished it was more of a comfort knowing so many people were right behind her. Yet it was all on her shoulders to make sure she and Mai stayed alive until everyone else could play their parts. The wrong word, or the twitch of an eye, and she and Mai could be dead before Steve and Al could rescue them.

Just the idea that her tiny granddaughter was involved was enough to make her cry. On one hand, she was glad that they'd be able to stop Ann Fletcher and Ray Quick. On the other hand, she wished the burglary ring would have decided to go anywhere but Charlotte.

She took a deep breath as she got closer to the stadium. It was starting to get dark, and the spotlights were coming on. Her heart was pounding as though she'd run a marathon, and her hands were cold and shaky on the steering wheel.

Come on, Peggy. Get yourself together. You have to be cool about this. Scared, of course, Ann would expect that. If you're too cool, she'll know there's a plan to thwart her. You can't give that away.

Peggy didn't usually drive past Panther's Stadium. She vaguely remembered that there were renovations going on there that wouldn't be finished until the fall when the football team played again. She hadn't realized how extensive the work was. There seemed to be scaffolding everywhere.

She parked her car in the visitors area. The construction crew was finished working for the day. There was no sign of Ann or Ray. She supposed they were somewhere they could see her, and tell if she'd been followed.

Peggy grabbed her handbag and locked the car, her eyes darting around the shadows where danger could be waiting. The sound of traffic zooming by on the Interstate blotted out the sound of her footsteps on the pavement.

She passed the construction trailer and skirted the keep-out barrier signs that would only keep out people who weren't intent on getting into the area. There was a small patch of half-dead spiraea struggling to survive in the midst of the chaos.

The weight of the jewelry in her bag seemed enormous, but she realized it was only her imagination.

Stay cool. Be calm. You can do this.

"Peggy! I was beginning to wonder if you were going to show up." Ray Quick jumped out of the shadows, forcing a small screech from her as she took a step back.

She put one hand to her throat. "For goodness sake, do you always have to be *so* dramatic?"

He laughed at her. "A scare is good for you. You and I are becoming friends now, aren't we?"

"Where is Ann?" Peggy didn't have time for his antics.

"She's waiting for you with that lovely daughter of yours. When is she due anyway? Looks like any minute."

"Never mind that. Let's get this over with."

Ray bowed and smiled at her. "After you, ma'am."

Peggy walked ahead of him past the cement mixers, forklifts, and supplies that were stacked haphazardly. She kept her eyes in front of her, focused on seeing Mai and Ann.

Ann was waiting with two other men under some scaffolding off to the left side of the entrance to the stadium. Peggy recognized her from her pictures, even though she'd aged. A dim light picked her out—and Mai seated on a pile of wood beside her.

"Dr. Peggy Lee." Ann moved toward her with her hand outstretched. "What a pleasure to finally meet you. I feel we're kindred spirits with our mutual interest in plants. I wish I would've felt comfortable coming up to you after the lecture, but things being what they are, I thought it best to make your acquaintance later. I knew we'd meet."

Peggy lightly touched her hand. "I have what you wanted. Now let Mai go."

"What about the money?" Ann picked up a leather case from the ground. "I thought you needed it."

"You're the one who made this personal by dragging my family into it." Peggy peeked at Mai. She seemed to be holding up in the situation. "All I wanted was the money and a clean exchange for the jewelry."

"Sorry to complicate matters, but I've been double-crossed before. You're right. I only want the jewelry. I stole it myself, you know? That was back at the beginning, before I had to pay that doctor at the hospital to put my name on Sheila's dead body. I had to leave it behind, but not by choice. I thought it was only fair that I should get it back after the mess Harry left me in."

"Is that why you killed him?"

"I'm sure you understand that he could identify me. I didn't want to run into him and have him start telling everyone that I was still alive. It was better this way. At least he knew what that I wasn't dead *before* he died."

Ann's smile was so smug that Peggy was glad she was part of sending this woman to prison. "I guess that was between you and Harry. I only came for Mai—and the money." Peggy took the jewelry out of her bag. "It's all yours."

"Aren't you curious about Arnie?" Ann asked.

"I assumed it was the same logic. Are we finished here?"

Ann's handsome face frowned. "I thought we could be friends, Peggy. I thought I could learn a few things from you. Using the lily of the valley poison has gotten old through the years. I know you understand, and you have information that could lead me into so much more."

Peggy raised her chin. "I don't tell people how to poison their friends and family. You'll just have to Google it."

"That's cold. I don't understand why you're so against helping me."

"I'm not a killer, Ann." Peggy walked over to where Mai was sitting and helped her to her feet. "I don't expect you to understand. You have what you wanted. We're leaving."

For a moment—Mai's trembling body pressed tightly to her side—Peggy thought they might just pull it off.

"What about the money?" Ann held out the leather

case again. "Don't forget that, or I might not trust you. That would be a pity."

Peggy had to leave Mai leaning against one of the metal legs that held the scaffolding above their heads. She took the case from Ann and started to walk away again.

"I don't know," Ann drawled. "I really *hate* for you to leave before I have a chance to pick your brain. Stay for a while, Peggy. Just let her go. You and I can talk. She was only to make sure you came alone. Let's be friends."

Mai bit her lips to hold in the small sob that almost escaped from her. She leaned heavily against Peggy. Ray tried to push between them to take the burden. Peggy pushed back at him. He banged at the scaffolding with a piece of pipe.

"I'm walking out of here with my daughter-in-law, Ann. You and I have nothing to talk about. Take what you came for, and go away."

In anger and frustration, Ray kicked at one of the posts that held the scaffolding. The whole set-up reverberated, "You're coming with us, Peggy. Let the mommy go now, before Ann changes her mind."

There wasn't much light, but Peggy heard a rumble above them before she noticed that the platform was shaking. The scaffolding appeared as though it was in the process of being taken down. It wasn't secure. The loose boards weren't anchored to the metal frame, as they should have been.

Ray's angry actions had started a chain reaction, causing the heavy boards above them to fall. She saw the metal post beside her buckle and threw herself and Mai on the ground.

Ann yelled a warning as a board fell and hit one of her men in the head. Several more boards dropped as Peggy was trying to maneuver her and Mai under the side of a cement mixer.

"I can't do this, Peggy," Mai sobbed. "I think the baby is coming."

"Not now," Peggy said. "Surely not *now*."

It was only another second before all of the boards were falling. Peggy saw one of them hit Ray and knock him to the ground. Dust and wood shavings flew everywhere. The sound of screws or nails pinged against metal. She kept Mai's head down.

Ann tried to move out of the way, but it was too late. A heavy board fell, hitting her in the leg and trapping her beneath the debris along with the rest of them. She let out an anguished scream.

Peggy was so busy trying to protect her and Mai from the falling wood and metal that she didn't realize it was over until the quiet broke through her concentration. "Mai? Are you okay?"

Mai panted hard. "I'm okay. But I'm definitely in labor. What are we going to do?"

Honeysuckle
Honeysuckle is native to the U.S. It may be the sweetest-smelling spring flower. The pretty yellow flowers on the climbing vine are beloved by hummingbirds—and can be a nuisance for gardeners. It has been used as various medicinals through the years, including fever reduction, infection arthritis, and the common cold.

Chapter Twenty-five

"Steve, Paul, and Al are here with us," Peggy whispered. "I'm sure they've called an ambulance by now. Just breathe. We'll be out of here in no time."

"Peggy? Mai?" Paul called out to them. "Are you okay?"

"We're doing okay down here," Peggy told him as Mai tried to breath through a contraction. "Please tell me you have an ambulance."

"On the way," Paul said. "Steve called the construction company. We can't pull you out of here without support. We're afraid the rest of the metal and wood will fall on you. Hold tight. I love you both."

It was quiet again, except for the sound of someone else that was trapped. It sounded like a man, moaning in pain. Peggy hoped it was Ray. She didn't care if it was a petty thing to wish.

The contraction passed. Mai took some cleansing breaths. "So they can't get us out of here? My baby is going to be born at a construction site?"

"I'm sure they'll get us out in time. For right now, lie back, and concentrate on your breathing. They'll have us out in no time."

Mai was able to do as Peggy suggested, until the next contraction. As the pain rippled through her, she yelled out and flailed her arms.

"Mai?" Paul called. "Is everything okay?"

"I'm having this *stupid* baby," Mai yelled back. "Get us out of here, Paul."

"We're doing the best we can," Steve replied. "You two take it easy in there. This whole mass is unstable. We need a few minutes to shore up the sides to pull you out."

"Hurry, Steve," Peggy said. "It's been a long time since I delivered a baby."

"I'm sure it's like riding a bicycle, sweetheart. You probably never forget how. We'll get you out as soon as we can."

"What about the others?" Peggy asked.

"We have Mrs. Fletcher and one of her accomplices," Steve told her. "Don't worry about them. You two just take care of each other."

Peggy knew that meant her taking care of Mai who was in no shape to care for anyone else. She encouraged her to breathe through her contractions that seemed to be coming very quickly. "How long has this been going on?"

"I've been down here a few hours," Mai replied. "I was about to call Paul, and go to the hospital when they came. It's been four or five hours since the contractions started. I think this may be it."

Peggy took a deep breath. She could hear work being done on the debris above them. She and Mai were fortunate that the wood had fallen in such a way that it had made a cave for them as it hit the cement mixer. They were at least partially protected from anything else hitting them.

Except sawdust.

Mai took in a deep breath and coughed as the dust flew around them. "Can't they do something about that? I'm trying to have a baby here."

"They're doing the best they can. Focus on what you're doing, and I'm sure Paul and Steve will have us out in no time."

She was saying the same thing an hour later as Mai's contractions got closer together. Maybe she should have started out saying they would be out that *night*. This way, her words of comfort rang hollow.

"Can you see anything?" Mai asked between contractions.

"Not yet." Peggy looked up at the wood and metal tented above them. It was completely dark now.

"Here it comes again," Mai groaned. "How close are they?"

Peggy glanced at her cell phone. "About two minutes apart. This could still go on for hours. It doesn't always happen fast."

"If you're trying to cheer me up, you're doing a *terrible* job."

There were some new voices above them. Two of them sounded urgent. And Vietnamese.

"That's my parents." Mai huffed between clenched teeth. "How did they find out about this? I wish they'd go back to the house and wait."

"Answer them," Peggy advised. "It's much better if they hear from you that you're okay."

Mai told her parents she was okay and then let out a loud scream. "Sorry, everyone. I just need to get this baby *out* of me."

"Everything is going well." Peggy tried to reassure those waiting outside. "The baby is coming."

Mai's parents shot back a rapid stream of words in Vietnamese.

"They're just worried," Paul said, understanding his wife's native tongue. "We'll take care of them, Mom. You two just work on the baby."

"There isn't anything else we *can* do," Mai grunted at him. "There better be donuts after this."

The contractions continued faster and harder. Peggy had some baby wipes in her bag that she used to smooth across Mai's perspiring face. "It won't be long now. Let's see if we can get you in a better position."

"My mother says that lying down to have a baby is stupid," Mai shot back. "She said she squatted to have me and my brother. She says the baby comes out faster that way."

Peggy eyed the wood above their heads. Mai was short, but she wasn't sure if she was short enough to squat under the debris. "I'll try to help you, if that's what you want."

"What are we going to put the baby in when she's born?" Mai moaned. "This place is filthy. Why am I having her *now*?"

"I don't have answers for all of that. But I'll take off my shirt, and we can catch the baby and wrap her in it. She won't touch the ground. I promise."

Peggy tried to help Mai squat to finish her labor, but it was difficult in the tight surroundings. Mai got into a sitting position, and then fell over as another contraction hit her. Peggy took off her shirt and got ready.

"Are you okay?" Steve asked. "You've been quiet for a minute or two."

"She's going to have the baby in here. Any progress out there?"

"They have a forklift that's going to move the bulk of the material that's over you. As soon as it gets here, I'll let you know so you can protect your heads. It's almost over,

Peggy. Hang on."

Peggy made herself face facts—she was going to deliver Mai's baby. She helped Mai lie down again, and parted the girl's legs to check on her progress. With the flashlight app on her cell phone, she checked how far along Mai was.

"I can see her head," she yelled to Mai, and everyone else listening. "Now's the time to push. Push hard, Mai. Your baby is coming."

Vietnamese mingled with shouts of joy and instructions from the paramedics who had arrived at the scene. Peggy helped Mai sit up and push with each contraction. English words became Vietnamese as Mai growled, cried, and screamed.

Peggy held her shirt in place so that the baby would come into her covered hands. She couldn't hold the cell phone at the same time, so she waited in the darkness until she felt the weight of the child.

"Why isn't she crying?" Mai demanded breathlessly. "She's *supposed* to cry."

Peggy lifted her new granddaughter and used her finger to clear the mucus from her nose and mouth. That was all it took. Mai and Paul's daughter let out a healthy wail that set up a cheer from everyone working outside. Peggy cried as she wrapped the shirt around the baby and carefully handed the tiny body to Mai.

"Okay, you two," Steve warned. "They're going to move some of the debris. Look out."

Peggy held her head down and arched her body across Mai's and the baby's. The forklift was loud and grating. The entire pile of wood and metal shifted as the long blades sank into it. As it moved back with its load, the forklift opened a hole right above their heads. The blades had barely cleared when rescue workers from the fire department snatched Peggy, Mai, and the baby out.

The night sky had never looked so beautiful to Peggy.

A whiff of honeysuckle washed over her. She knew it wasn't possible—honeysuckle flowers were long gone for the season. Maybe it was her heart, feeling as light as spring.

She snuggled her face into Steve's neck as he held her close to him.

"Nice look." He put his jacket around her bare shoulders. "Are you okay?"

"Better than okay." She grinned. "I'm a grandma."

* * *

Paul rode in the ambulance with Mai and their baby. Peggy allowed the paramedics who were there to check her, but she knew she wasn't hurt. She refused a ride to the hospital for further testing.

Ann and her gang had survived the accident and been rounded up by Al to take them to the county jail. There were a few words between Steve and Al about jurisdiction, but everyone was feeling too good to let that get in the way. Peggy had promised them both a detailed account of everything that had happened before the scaffolding had fallen.

She and Steve were the last to arrive at the hospital. It wasn't easy, but Steve convinced Peggy to go home, take a shower, and get dressed. By the time they reached the maternity floor, Mai's parents, and Peggy's parents, were already admiring the new addition to their families through the large natal window.

Peggy's mother stared at her. "I can't believe all of us got here to see your granddaughter before *you*. What in the world have you been doing that was so much more important?"

Steve put his arm around Peggy. She smiled, grateful to see her granddaughter's rosy little face through the window.

"Just messing around, as usual, Mom." Peggy wiped tears from her green eyes. "You know how I am."

Epilogue

Peggy had gone to bed at a little past midnight, but she couldn't sleep. Steve had left to work out the details of the gang's arrest with Al. She thought that would probably take most of the night.

Shakespeare stayed with her as she went downstairs. The plants in the basement beckoned, as always, but there was something else she wanted to see for herself.

She and Walter had put the boxes into the library that they'd taken from the storage unit. She thought about Arnie as she wandered into the room and switched on the light.

Before leaving the hospital, she'd seen him. His doctor said that he believed Arnie was going to pull through, though it had been touch and go for him. He was on a respirator, unconscious, but she'd squeezed his hand and kissed his cheek.

The boxes were dusty and crammed with pens, pencils, newspaper clippings, and old notes. She was searching for the files that Paul said he'd seen when he'd stolen everything from the mini-storage. It was silly, but she wanted to read them. Whatever they said was part of her past—part of her life with John.

She found the files that were filled with documents describing Ann's 'death' and Harry's investigation, but there were no files about John.

Puzzled, she searched more carefully through the boxes, pulling everything out. The files Paul had found had disappeared. She paused and thought a moment.

Where could they have gone?

She looked a third time, but the files simply weren't in the boxes she'd brought home.

A noise at the door startled her.

It was Steve. "Aren't you asleep yet?" He smiled and took her hand. "I thought you wouldn't wake up until morning after everything you've been through."

"You know I'm not the greatest sleeper." She got to her feet. "I can't find the files Harry said were in here about John."

"Maybe he was lying," Steve said. "Maybe he never had them in the first place."

"I don't think so—" She didn't want to tell him about Paul's actions.

He tugged at her hand. "Come on. Let's go to bed. We can figure it out tomorrow."

Peggy switched off the light, and went with him. Paul had copies of those files, she reminded herself. She could read those.

But what had happened to the originals?

She got in bed with Steve, and he put his arm around her. "You know, it might be for the best that Harry didn't have those files about John," he said. "It couldn't make much difference now. You should move past it, Peggy."

She didn't answer, but long after Steve's breathing had slowed as he slept, she was awake, wondering.

Peggy's Garden Journal

Fall is an important time in the garden. Not only is it a good time for planting trees, shrubs, and spring bulbs—it's a good time to take stock of your yard and make plans for the year.

Frequently, gardeners are too busy in spring and summer to really form a plan on what they'd like to do with what they have. Not having a plan can cost you in plant mistakes such as the bushes you put by the front windows that are too large now to see out.

Consider making a map of your garden. Fill in every plant you have, along with their heights and growth cycles. Remember that you'd like to have something colorful or blooming, even in the winter.

Always take this with you when you shop for plants so you can refer to it before you buy anything. A good garden plan will save you time and money, and you'll be happier with your yard!

Happy Gardening!

Peggy

My favorite recipe for onion soup
8 servings

The key to great onion soup is to cook the onions thoroughly, but slowly. They should be sweet, dark, and soft when finished. I use a vegetable broth instead of chicken stock. Garnish with cheese, and serve with toasted French bread.

3 Tbs. butter

1 Tbs. vegetable oil

7 to 8 cups thinly sliced (or chopped if you like) onions

Salt to taste

2 Tbs. all-purpose flour

6 cups low-sodium vegetable broth (6 cubes of stock with 6 cups of hot water)

1 tsp. chopped fresh thyme or ½ tsp. dried

¼ tsp. freshly ground pepper

10 to 12 oz. shredded Gruyere cheese

In large, heavy pot, melt 2 tablespoons butter with oil over medium heat. Stir in onions, and seasonings. Cook 1 minute, stirring constantly. Reduce heat, cover and cook 10 minutes. Remove lid and cook 15 minutes more, stirring occasionally. Add remaining butter to pot. Cook, stirring occasionally, until onions are caramelized and very soft, about 15 minutes.

Stir in flour and cook 3 to 4 minutes. Stir in broth. Cover and simmer 15 minutes.

Ladle soup into an ovenproof crock or bowl. Sprinkle with cheese. Broil until cheese is bubbly and golden. Serve hot.

Edible plants in your garden

Many gardeners are replacing flowering plants with edible ones. Tomatoes, peppers, garlic, and onions are all popular annual replacement plants.

But did you know that you probably already have edible plants in your yard?

Bachelor's button flowers are edible. So are bee balms, marigold, and carnations. Dandelions are delicious greens and nasturtium flowers add spice. You can also eat rose petals and violets. Crushed in drinks or served with food, they can add color and unique flavor to your meals.

One caution: NEVER eat flowers from plants you don't know, or pick flowers from forests or alongside the road. Grow the plants yourself to be sure what you're getting.

Botanical poisons can be deadly!

About the Authors

Joyce and Jim Lavene write bestselling mystery together. They have written and published more than 70 novels for Harlequin, Berkley and Gallery Books along with hundreds of non-fiction articles for national and regional publications.

Pseudonyms include J.J. Cook, Ellie Grant, Joye Ames and Elyssa Henry

They live in rural North Carolina with their family, their rescue animals, Quincy - cat, Stan Lee - cat and Rudi - dog. They enjoy photography, watercolor, gardening and long drives

Visit them at www.joyceandjimlavene.com

Facebook: www.Facebook.com/JoyceandJimLavene

Twitter: https://twitter.com/AuthorJLavene

Amazon Author Central Page:
http://amazon.com/author/jlavene

Made in the USA
San Bernardino, CA
27 November 2017